The Hidden Truth

Ethan Vale

Contents

PROLOGUE

T ing!

And the elevator opened. All heads on the hallway turned around to see who it was. Even though the gap was small, everybody knew who's in it. Of course, who can miss the same familiar outfit. The outfit of death and pure evil. Black shoes, black pants, black coat and tie and a white shirt barely noticeable since it is hidden under a black vest.

That's Mr. Black, A man who dresses like somebody died. Mr. Black is not a nickname given to him for the way he dress but it's actually his real name which complements the way he dress.

Everybody turned in their panicky state. Someone ran to the bathroom and closed the door while somebody cursed for not being able to sprint first. Neil opted to hide under his table and the Polasky sisters together with some others went for the canteen.

Believe me when I say that that all happened in a few second because the time when the elevator door completely opened, everyone pretended to be very busy. Everybody was focusing on something else like random documents as if they were busy reading it or on their computers while typing keys at random. Nosy Kate chose to staple blank papers. Everyone becomes creative when Mr. Black arrives. No two people should be doing the same excuse or it would become obvious that they're acting kind of odd.

I, for instance froze when he started to walk towards his office. It's been a week since I started working here but I still feel like a coconut just fell on my head. Mr. Black scanned the whole area. Feeling satisfied, he continued on walking.

I stood up once he was near my table and did my part on the routine.

"Good morning sir." I greeted. As usual he didn't say anything or even react on my remark. Once his office door was closed, everyone heaved a sigh of relief including me. No one was fired today. It must be our lucky day or our boss is in a good mood.

For the week that I stayed here, 10 people were fired for silly reasons and that includes staring blankly at the wall, standing on the hallway (and blocking his way), ugly shoes, laughing in the office and many more. Only the upper and some middle management are safe from Mr. Black's wrath.

Some long term employees often joke that I should be the next one to lose my job since the position of Mr. Black's personal assistant and I quote, 'has been and ever will be replaceable'. A betting pool was even created in my honor and a month being the longest.

Even with Mr. Black's cold attitude I enjoyed working here. The employees have got this instant bond to everyone since our favorite topic to talk about during our break is our personal encounter with Mr. Black and how scared we felt during that encounter.

If you're wondering why there's never a shortage of employee it's because the pay here is good. So good that I decided to leave my old job as a waiter and move here in the city.

I was born and raised outside the city but last week while I was doing my usual job as a waiter, someone offered me to work here in this company and gave me a business card. He promised that the pay would be good and here I am now. Working as a personal assistant for Mr. Black.

The intercom buzzed. Mr. Black was calling me from his office. I stood up and immediately went inside his office.

"Yes, sir?"

"I want you to sort this file according to their pages and please inform Mr. Castillo that I can't meet him today." As usual, he was in his cold demeanor. I started to pick-up the pieces of papers on the floor as careful as possible so as not to crumple them. I know I don't have a right to say this but man, he is a man of order. How clumsy of him to scatter the pages of this file.

I picked up almost every pages except for the ones that are under his table. His table is different from the typical desks since it's made of glass and it doesn't have that cover in front of his legs. I started to crawl towards the remaining sheets until I realized that I was facing his crotch.

"Ahem! What are you doing?" I looked up and I saw that he was looking at me. Damn this transparent table.

"Uhm... I-I was retrieving the remaining pages!" The squeak at the end of my sentence is not helping either. He might think that I'm a pervert!

"Can't you do it without staring at my crotch?" How did he even know I was staring at it? He was busy writing something a while ago. Not unless he got this ultra genitalia sensor that senses if somebody was staring at his dick- which I never did mind you.

"I'm not staring at it!" I replied. I can't tell you how weird this conversation is that is why I decided to just pick everything up and to get the hell out of his table.

Once I got out of his office, I repeatedly slap my face for that awkward encounter. I should be thankful he didn't fire me on the spot.

Chapter 1

Who in their right mind would not staple, bind, or clip a 400+ pages of annual report? Because of that I have to arrange the pages that my boss have jumbled.

I had only arranged the first 20 pages of the report when the intercom buzzed again.

"Flynn! Where's my godamn coffee?" Mr. Black demanded. Oh no. I totally forgot! It's 9:00 and it's time for his morning coffee.

"In a minute sir." I replied and I immediately went straight for the elevator. Gosh darn. I lost track of time! The coffee shop is just in front of the building but it would take me 10 minutes tops to get the coffee and return to my office.

Once I reached the ground floor, I sprinted towards the coffee shop not minding all the honking of the cars that I just passed.

"Hey! Get in line!""Bastard!""Wait for your turn you spoiled corporate brat!"

That was just some of the insults I heard from the people in line. I am not actually used to cutting in line but my needs are bigger right now.

"The usual coffee for Mr. Black." I said to the crew. He nods and started to brew. The workers already know how to make Mr. Black's coffee. They have been making the same coffee and giving it to different assistants for years. That's why they understand my need to cut in line.

I am soaking wet once I reached our floor. It looks like I just took a shower from all the sweat that is dripping down my forehead. All heads are looking at me now like they're watching an interesting movie. Am I on the climax? Is this the day I'm finally be fired?

"H-here's your c-coffee sir." My hand was shaking from stress and also nervousness.

"You're 12 minutes late." He answered casually.

"Better late than never." I smiled even though he is not looking at me.

He did not reply. I don't know what to do. Should I give it to him or leave the coffee at his table? I honestly don't know. I was about to leave the coffee on his table when he spoke.

"Throw it." Wait. What? I frickin got this coffee for him. I wiped the sweat from my face hoping he would notice my hardships in getting his coffee. "Didn't you hear me? I said no longer need the damn coffee."

Fine. He's the boss.

"Yes sir I understand." I went out of his office with the coffee in my hand. Whatever. It's his money anyway.

It was already 4:00 but Mr. Black is not coming out of his office. That's odd since he was never been a second late to his meetings. I tried to call him but he is not picking up.

My fingers started to tap the table. He's gonna be late for his meeting. Clearly something is wrong.

I've made my decision and that is to barge in his office even though he warned me not to go there without his permission. I don't want to be blamed if he'll be late for his meeting.

I've knocked but still there's no answer. That leaves me no choice so I pushed the door slowly and peeked inside

Mr. Black was leaning on the table. I was worried at first but then I realized that he was just sleeping. Okay. This is awkward. How do I wake him?

I stood beside him and it was the first time that I saw him without his cold demeanor. It was like he's just a normal guy. A different man from my stoic boss. I never wanted to wake him but I'm gonna face hell if I didn't. And so, I started to poke him in the arm but he's still sleeping. I'm still thinking on the way I'm gonna wake him without pissing him off.

"Sir..." I shook him slightly and he opened his eyes.

"What time is it?" He asked me and he was back. The frosty Mr. Black.

"Uhmm." I looked into my watch and replied, "It 4:05 pm sir." I smiled hoping that he will not get mad at me again.

"Fuckin Christ! This is what happens when I miss my morning coffee!"Sadly that was just wishful thinking. "We only have 25 minutes left. Why only now?" He's now fixing himself and started to stand up. "Hmmm?" He was looking at me straight in the eyes but I cannot respond since I felt my throat closing up.

"I-I tried calling you sir but I cannot reach you" I stammered. "I-I thought you were busy and I couldn't go into your office since you ordered me not to come without your permission sir." I attempted to return his stare but something about his gaze makes me feel like my soul is burning.

Tic. Toc. Tic. Toc.

Silence. He's not saying anything. Why won't he say anything?

Tic. Toc. Tic. Toc.

He just grunted and started to walk away. I was left catching my breath. His intensity is just extreme. Once I recovered from his death stare, I trotted my way outside and followed him. He was already in the elevator. Mr. Black saw me but instead of stopping the elevator he pressed the close button. Luckily I caught up with him and slipped my fingers inside before the doors have closed. I can't tell you how awkward it is in the elevator. Nobody spoke a single word or even made a sound. The only sound that you can hear is the sound of the conveyor descending.

I don't know if it's my imagination but I can see that he was looking at my reflection. Our reflections was distorted by the metal door but I can feel that he was still staring at me. It was only when the doors that opened that I was interrupted from my reverie. As usual he went out first and I was left following him like a loyal dog.

His driver was already waiting and he opened the door for Mr. Black before going to the driver's seat. I sat in front of Mr. Black and my suspicion was confirmed when I noticed that he was still staring at me. What the heck is his problem? I kept my head down to avoid the stare of death but it was just damn annoying because I can feel that he's still scrutinizing me. I decided to confront him but the moment that our eyes have met, I was taken into a new dimension. I lost my senses and my ability to speak has been taken away. A familiar memory was coming back to me. It's funny because the moment I looked into Mr. Black's eyes I involuntarily remembered someone from my past that I buried into my memories a long time ago.

It can't be possible because they are not the same person. But I don't know why some shrouded memories are starting to resurface.

Chapter 2

I went home both physically and mentally exhausted.

From the boring meeting and the memory surge, I sure wanted to just lie down and sleep. I just wonder... why did I suddenly remember him? The same familiar ache is coming back again. It's history but it's still painful like it was just yesterday.

I decided to just forget what happened and focus more on my job. I don't want Mr. Black to call me lazy and incompetent again but this time a girl who I've never saw before is attempting to go into his office. Mr. Black made it clear with me a hundred times to never let anyone into his office unless they are written on his schedule. He also stated that even though they will tell me that they are important people or even the president I'm gonna have to stop them from 'disturbing' his office hours.

"Uhmm. Excuse me miss, I'm afraid I'm gonna have to stop you right there." fair enough she stopped from her tracks and started to approach my table.

"Oh. You're new. what's your name?" She was one of the prettiest girl I have ever seen but her fake voice ruined it for me.

"I'm Michael Flynn. I'm sorry ma'am but I don't recognize you. I believe you are not scheduled to see Mr. Black."

"I'm here to see Magnus." she's very confident. Of course with her voluptuous body and her sophisticated clothes who wouldn't be?

"Who?" I replied.

"Oh my gosh. I'll pretend I didn't hear that since you're new. I'm Maddison. Don't you worry about me I'm here to see my darling dearest." and she winked at me before jostling herself into Mr. Black's office.

"Oh no. no. no." I held her arm before she could even take a step closer to my boss. I already despise this woman. She's pretentious and tries to act like cute little child even though she looks like she already spawned a dozen of child. Plus I'm sensing a little bit of a bitchy attitude hidden in plain sight. I know a bitch when I see one. I learned that when I was still a waiter.

"Let me go!" she was forcing herself to be free and her annoying lengthy nails have scratched my neck repeatedly. Our little tussle ended when Mr. Black spoke without even looking to any of us.

"It's alright Flynn." said Mr. Black and this woman child looked at me with her I told you so look.

"Okay Sir." I stated before closing the door. She called him Magnus. Does that mean that Magnus Black is the full name of Mr. Black? That's like new information to me. I know it's a shame to just discover your boss's complete name when you've been working for him for a couple of weeks now but everyone in the office calls him Mr. Black. I didn't bother to even ask what his full name was which is even more embarrassing.

That realization pushed me to search his name on the internet because it made me realize that I don't know shit about my boss and that's just sad especially when I'm his personal assistant.

Magnus Black

Then search. It's not so difficult to find him since he was the top result which is actually impressive. I decided to click one of the articles that caught my attention.

Attractive Businessmen That Will Surely Make You Thirssstyyy

Psssh. Typical Buzzfeed Article.

Number 10... Meh not important. I just scrolled my way to the link while focusing only on the pictures. Although I can say that they are all good looking, only number 1 and 2 are above them all. And it's not surprising that Mr. Black is on the top.

Number 1: Magnus Josef BlackHeight: 6'1Age: 28Occupation: CEO of Black IndustriesLikes: Golf, Caviar, good liquors, trading, Yacht, polo, watchesStatus: In a relationship

Eh. Typical rich people can only afford. I'm pertaining about his likes.

What to know about Magnus:

• Graduated Summa Cum Laude at Harvard University

• Finished his masters degree at Standford Graduate School of Business

• The first born son of Mr. Bennett Black, founder of Black Industries.

• Was offered to be a model and an actor but declined to become both.

• In a relationship with runway model Madison Brooke.

That's actually impressive. Now I'm starting to have second thoughts about my boss.

What turns you on?A pretty face.

That's it? He gave the shortest answer among those that were interviewed. He should learn from Number 2 because he said: Someone who cares for me, a beautiful heart, attracted to intellect. Spot on! It should be like that. Affected or not we should be attracted to other things rather than superficial things and I am not saying this because I'm not attractive but because... Okay I admit, I'm affected because some people like us are not received well in the general public hence it's harder for us to find even a fling.

Why did you go into business?I was born with it. I might as well die with it.

What kind of answer is this?

Give me a thing that you hate?This interview. (Don't know if it's a joke since Mr. Black said this with a straight face)

Oh god. Typical Mr. Black.

CHAPTER 3

The door suddenly opened and I instantly closed all the tabs on the browser. If I am caught browsing on the internet while stalking my boss, it would be both awkward and at the same time irresponsible since I am breaking a company law.

"We're going out for lunch." He said as a matter of fact but that statement alone deviates what's written on his planner.

"But sir..."

"You know the drill." Before I could even inquire he snaked his arm around Maddison and the woman child inclined her head towards Mr. Black and started to giggle like a little girl who was just given a candy.

Fine. The drill. Cancel, Reschedule, Forestall.

A few minutes after they have left, a man in a suit approached my table.

"I'm here to see Mr. Black." I looked up and saw a man with the same age group as Mr. Black. He sure does look familiar. I think I saw him before somewhere.

"And you are?" I asked with a smile like I used to when I asked people of they would like to eat.

"I'm Hector." he replied.

Hector... Is it possible that...

"Hector Mason." he repeated when he noticed that I was suddenly preoccupied.

"Oh yes. Mr. Mason." I said when I saw his name on Mr. Black's calendar.

"I'm sorry but Mr. Black is out of the office right."

"Oh is that so?" he asked amused and went ahead to open Mr. Black's office. Ugh. Why do people never believe me. Is barging in to Mr. Black's office the norm here? I was not informed.

"Wow! I didn't notice that Mr. Black is in his office right now. He must be a magician!" I exclaimed sarcastically. First that woman child and now him.

"Fine! I'm sorry but I have a scheduled meeting with him today. And I know how he usually makes excuses to cancel his meetings."

"I"m sorry too for being unprofessional. It's just that you're the second person who tried to claw his way in to Mr. Black's office this day." I apologized since I realized he must be some important person and I acted in a childish way.

"It's fine really I know that you're just doing what you're told to do. By the way, where is he?"

"He's with his girlfriend. Would you like to wait?"

"Ahhh. Madison. Yeah sure. I need to talk to him."

I offered him to take a seat and asked if he wants anything like coffee or water but he said no. He just sat down and kept himself busy with his phone. I continued to rearrange the annual summary report that Mr. Black gave to me yesterday and I'm still on page 263 when he approached my table. He probably got bored or something. I mean who wouldn't? It's almost an hour when he got here.

"It's a bit weird but you're the first male secretary he ever had." he said in a way that it means something.

"And your point being?" I bit my tongue for the second time. Damn. I can't stop myself from being tactless. I should stop my habit of talking like I'm still a waiter who needs to deal with unreasonable people. "It's not Mr. Black who hired me. It was... a middle aged man." I realized I didn't know the name of the one who recruited me here. I just know his face but not his name. Everything happened so fast.

"Hmm. Interesting, I usually see different girls in your chair probably every week."

"Did you know that your name sounds like a famous pornstar?"

"Haha. Funny. You're not the first person who said that to me."

He is a friendly man, I can feel it but there's something about him like I've seen him before. It's not like he is...

"That's it! You're Hector Mason!" I cried when I laid my eyes on my computer.

"Yeah. I said my name a while ago. Are you that slow?" he replied jokingly.

"No. I mean the Hector Mason who is looking for a beautiful heart and is attracted to intellect." He thought about this for a second until he chuckled.

"Oh God. Attractive businessmen that will surely make you thirstyyy. I didn't know you're into that kind of articles. Crap! I remembered when that article came out, hundreds of fanmail flooded my office for the whole month." he was laughing when he recalled the article that I just read.

"Not to hurt your ego but I just read that article because I was doing some research about Mr. Black." I retorted.

"And why is that may I ask? Do you have a crush on your boss ey?" he winked at me and wiggled his eyebrows like I have some major crush on Mr. Black. Fuck no!

"The f? No I don't. I just realized I never know shit about my boss when Madison mentioned his first name." I don't have a boss complex fetish. I'm fuckin asexual!

"Really? No! You're kidding me. Everybody knows who Magnus is." when he saw me being serious he sounded more shocked than before. "What? Really? He has a high profile relationship with Madison and a presentable face on the media."

"So are you saying that the both of you are famous? I don't believe that businessmen are even famous to the masses not unless you're in a novel or a movie." Or maybe Bill Gates or Mark Zuckerburg but they are not considered as celebrities.

"Have you seen Magnus? He looks like a movie star. Who doesn't love attractive people with money? He's actually very popular to ladies with daddy issues."

I took a second look at him from head to foot.

"Yo! Are you saying that I'm not atttactive?" he asked and flashed his killer smile to me.

"That's not my point. I am not really attracted to anyone. Besides, I grew up in the country. Away from the city. There's more important things than knowing who's famous or not. You keep yourself busy by surviving. Life's that simple."

Based on his expression, he looks like he just heard something interesting. Goodness rich people. Maybe I should build a theme park wherein I charge a load of bucks to rich people so that they can experience the humdrum life of being poor.

"Okay..." he said in surrender.

I heard the beeping of the elevator indicating that Mr. Black is here. True enough he came out with Madison on his side, her hands wrapped around his right arm.

"Hey Magnus! How dare you cancel your appointment with me?" Hector greeted them in a cheerful manner but Mr. Black does not look pleased. When did he looked happy? Maybe never. His heart is made of stone.

"Something important came up." he replied flatly.

"Ohoho. Sure sure. Hello Maddy!"

"Hi! Looking good there Hector."

"Hey Magnus, you'll never believe what your sercretary told me." I turned my attention to them because I became the subject of their conversation but before I could even listen to their conversation they already went inside Mr. Black's office. Dammit!

Chapter 4

I once met a man named Hector. It was so long ago and the memory of him seems like a blur to me. I can't recall what he look like exactly but he plays a big part on my teenage life that I still remember his name.

The river flows calmly in Carmona Rosa. It's always been that way except for the times when hurricane comes. I saw a man sitting beside the deciduous tree. The color of yellow and orange emerging among the green grasses.

I called him. He looks back but all I can see is the sparkling water reflecting the light of the sun. Then everything went black. I am now standing in front of a casket. A coffin which contains the body of my dead mother. I went forward. Every step I take feels like I am walking on quicksand. It feels like I am being pulled into the earth. And when I can finally see my lifeless mother, she reached out to me and held my hand.

I opened my eyes and inhaled as much air as I can. My body feels warm and I already know that I have been sweating profusely. I looked at the time and the clock says it's 4:37 am. Way early than my alarm clock. I decided to get up. Drink some water and take a shower. It's been years since I had a nightmare.

I looked at my run-downed face. I opened the tap and washed my exhausted looking face. Today is another day.

Once I stepped off the elevator, I can see my coworkers looking at me. What's the matter? They were looking at me like I'm off to Calvary. When I finally reached my desk, I finally knew the reason. Mr. Black is here inside his office.

Early.

And that never happened before. I started to go through my files. I checked his calendar. He is not scheduled this early. What did I miss? Should I let him know that I'm here? As if on cue the telephone rang.

"Yes sir?" I said. Somehow his early admission is making me nervous.

"I need the annual report now." now that he's on the phone. He sounds like a robot more than ever.

"Certainly sir." I grabbed the compiled and arranged annual report and started to walk into his office. Good thing I finished it yesterday. You'll never know when he needed something. If he says he need it now, you need to give it fast even if it means selling your soul to the devil.

I took a deep breath before pushing the matted glass door into his office.

"Here you go sir." I left the compiled annual report on his table. He did not react or said anything so I started to walk on my way out when he called my name.

"I'm not yet done with you Flynn." his voice which seemed like a growl made me flinch in surprise.

"Yes sir? Do you need anything?" I asked.

"Please have a seat." he pointed on the chair in front of his desk. Is this how he fires his employees? Did the time finally came where I made a mistake? I sat down and tried to look at him but I focused my gaze on his back instead.

"Do you recall what you said to Mr. Mason yesterday?" he inquired like I'm in a police investigation.

"I've said many things Sir." is this related to what Hector said to him before the door have closed?

"Didn't you mention to him that his name sounds like a famous pornstar?"

"Yes sir."

"I mean why would you say that?" his voice sounds serious than normal. He's angry. The beast is angry

"I don't know sir. I mean... it was supposed to be a joke which he took lightly." that was close. One of his most hated reply is the phrase 'I don't know.' "It's unprofessional! You directly insulted one of my clients." I averted   my stare. Fuck. I can feel my body weakening. I want the earth to take me down.

"I'm sorry sir. I promise that this will never happen again." I stammered as a last resort. I didn't know what to do or say. The beast is angry.

He didn't say anything for a minute. I didn't know what to do or say. He was just staring at me. Scrutinizing every movement I make.

"You better fucking don't." he finally said. "By the way where's the second copy of this that I wanted you to print?"

What second copy?

"When did you tell me to photocopy the file sir?" I have to chose my questions wisely or else I'm gonna be annihilated again.

"So you're telling me you're not reading your emails?"

Emails? I checked all my emails before going home.

"I'm opening all my emails before checking out sir."

"Well, check again. Are you telling me that I'm a liar?" he said sarcastically.

"No Sir. I'll check again, Sir." I replied before finding the right time to get out of his office.

Upon checking my email there was indeed an attachment from my boss. Only thing is that, he sent it after my office hours. So he expects me to check my emails at all times. I don't even have a sufficient money to afford a decent apartment in the city and yet he expects me to have the luxury of having data or internet to check my emails. Does he knows that I don't even have the time to open my Facebook?

I opened the file and squinted my eyes in annoyance. He made me arrange a whole lot of pages when he could've just let me print a copy of it. Well sure it's a waste of paper and money but you know...

I started to print the file. The only thing that's left to do is watch as the printer produces every page that's done and reproduced. I gave my full attention too much attention on the matter that I never noticed that I was looking at a newly printed annual report for god knows how long.

I took the duplicate and placed it in a folder before going back to Mr. Black's office. First name Magnus. Like the famous brand of condom? No that's Magnum but whatever Maybe that's the reason why he's so sensitive with names. Dammit. What am I thinking?

Maybe I should just stop meddling with other people's name just because my name is so generic.

"I have the second copy, Sir." I announced once I entered beast's dungeon.

"Then it's time to take a trip." he stood up and put on his black coat. He took bunch of document and gave them to me in surprise that I dropped some of them.

"Clumsy." he commented as I pick up the documents on the floor.

As usual, he left me again and started to walk ahead but I caught up with him before he tries to ride the elevator by himself again. As if!

The driver is already waiting for us and opened the door for Mr. Black. I sat on my usual place just in front of him. I bowed my head like I normally do but I then heard him call my name.

"Mr. Flynn... You've been my assistant for how long? Two weeks?" he asked. Is he trying to make a conversation?

"Yes sir." I replied.

"Okay. So where are you from?"

I turned to him and he was again staring at me intently. That's how he normally speaks to people but I can't seem to get used to it. I feel like I'm talking to a stranger. He had this stoic expression and a commanding voice. I've never met someone who's intimidating as him.

"I grew up from a little place called Carmona Rosa. Had a little family business there before moving to Arbington."

"And your family business?"

"A bed and breakfast place. There was a river and a lake near our house where people usually visits. It wasn't much but it still helps with the bills."

"So why'd you move here in the city?"

"We sold our house because..." I paused for a moment to compose myself. I can feel my stomach regurgitating. "It's a long story. Anyway, we can't pay the expenses anymore. The mortgages, taxes, the operating costs to run a business. My father decided to sell the house and to move to a smaller place."

There was silence for a minute and I thought that he's done talking to me but he asked me a question again.

"Why did you choose to work in my company?"

"Uhmm. Well it's kind of weird actually. Somebody posted what I did on Facebook. There was this homeless man who was begging for food on the restaurant I work for. I was a waiter back then. I invited him inside and ordered some food for him using my own money. Apparently somebody saw me and took a picture of what I did. The next thing I knew I was being interviewed for the late night news."

Mr. Black's eyebrows crinkled indicating that he's either angry or confused. Maybe he's thinking about the why am I telling that story.

"Don't worry it's important to the plot." I said as an assurance. "And then one day, a balding middle aged man dined into the resto. He recognized me from the news and invited me to work in your company. He must be the HR or something cause I didn't see him during my interview. He said he admires me for my compassion and sympathy and that he wants me to work at Black Industries. After discussing what I could get if I work in you comapny, I made a decision to move here. So there..."

He nodded as a response. The awkward silence is back. I heard the sounds of horns blowing from the nearby cars. There was a loud crash and the car suddenly halted to a stop.

I was thrown off my seat and I unexpectedly found myself in between Mr. Black's legs. My hands on his knees.

Gaddemmit! What's the deal with his crotch? I instantly removed my hand from his knees and returned to seat. Fuck! Fuck! Fuck! I should wear my seatbelt at all times. It's not like I intended that to happen. Maybe I should just say no homo and everything will be alright.

"Are you alright Sir?" the driver inquired to my boss. I'm not okay. Why didn't he asked me? "Some drunk biker crashed his motor to the auto in front of us." he explained.

"We're fine. Is the road blocked?"

"No sir. Cars can still pass through the side."

"Good. Find another route if you have to."

"Copy that sir." the driver said before closing the divider.

"So uhmm." shit. What's a good excuse for my fucking embarass-ment? I started to clear my throat hoping for some magic words to come out of my mouth. I was once again face to face and in close promximity to his groin.

"Use your damn seatbelt the next time we take a ride. I'm starting to think you want to suck my dick."

Chapter 5

It's so hard to breathe or even concentrate on what's happening because I almost touched Mr. Black's you-know-what. Yeah sure he's attractive as fuck but I'm not gay!

If I strain my neck from staring out my window then let it be. I don't think I even have a face left after what happened.

After an agonizing trip, we finally arrived in a very expensive looking restaurant. The valet opened the door of the limousine. I followed Mr. Black as he entered the premises. I don't usually go with him during meetings except if I had to do some boring trivial stuff like taking notes or becoming a proxy for him when the meeting gets boring.

Mr. Black walked graciously along the corridor while all the staffs are distancing themselves to the side like the parting of the red sea. Amazing how his demeanor can scare people even though they are not his employees. Or is it? Maybe this was indeed one of his business. All I know is that Mr. Black is a filthy rich bastard who owns a lot of business establishments.

He declared a name to the receptionist, which I didn't catch, and we were escorted to a table where a man in his forties is waiting.

"Magnus Black." he regarded when we finally reached his table.

"Mr. Sheppard. It's nice to finally meet you." Magnus replied as he took the hand of the other man to shake it.

So here's what happened. I don't wanna bore you with the details cause I am already bored with the long talk. Mr. Black wanted to merge one of his company, Accelerate, to Mr. Sheppard's Amplify. The proposal is that Accelerate would absorb Amplify and will be in charge of the production, marketing and distribution of the product and Mr. Sheppard will receive a 30% cut of the total net income of Accelerate in the region. On the other hand Mr. Sheppard wants to have a consolidation, a dissolution of both companies in order to create a new one with a share 40% of the gross income.

Of course Mr. Black wasn't pleased with the demand because first, Accelerate is a global brand so it can't possibly be dissolved to sacrifice for a possible consolidation. Second, the only purpose of the merger is that Mr. Black wants to have a bigger market share in Oakridge since Mr. Sheppard literally rules all the shoe stores in the region. If you can't beat them, join them. I don't know but that's what I got from the long talk. The things I learn in the industry even though I didn't have a business degree.

"So you're telling me, the merger only applies to your stores in all Oakridge and I only get a 30% of the net income?" Mr. Sheppard repeated.

"We checked the numbers. It's good. You don't have to work anymore. You can have a perpetual vacation and let us do all the work." Mr Black countered.

"It's like you bought my company but not really. If sales plummets, I am also affected. And I can't do anything about it since I can't interfere with the management! This is acquisition in disguise!"

"Have you ever seen one of our business failing? I don't think so." Mr. Black is starting to sound annoyed.

"Yeah. But what if this is just a ploy to lose one of your competition? You deliberately fail the business and you can easily start a new one."

"If that's the case then we'll fail together and you should know that I don't accept failure."

"Nope. I still don't trust you. If you really are a global company, why is it that you are so interested to be our partner company?"

Do I need to write this? I stopped writing when things got personal for the last minute.

"We can beat you if want you know. We can lower the price of our products at a break-even level until you lose all your customers. Walmart can do it to small business enterprises. So do we."

"Ha! Let's see, our customers are loyal to us. There is a reason why they call me the king of Oakridge. I fuckin own the market!"

"Why don't you ask my assistant. He's originally from Oakridge."

I was taken by surprise when Mr. Black included me in their conversation. Is this why he decided to invite me in their meeting? He asked me a while ago where I grew up. He knows what he's doing this sneaky bastard.

"Oh really? From where were you?" Mr. Shellard asked suddenly interested in what I have to say.

"I grew up in Carmona Rosa."

"Oh! The home of the red river. So what brings you here in the big city?" he sounded really excited. Did Mr. Black anticipate this? It's like I rehearsed what I'm going to say this very moment.

"It's a long story actually but to cut it short, we had a small bed and breakfast place but we couldn't pay the bills anymore. That's why my father decided to move into a smaller place." I replied trying not to remember the real reason why we gave up the place.

"So what can you say about Amplify products?" Mr. Black interjected. I looked at him with with a stupefied look on my face. Where's he going with this? He nudged my leg with his to indicate that I should speak immediately or else he's gonna kill me.

"Well it's the number one preffered brand in Oakridge when it comes to footwears. You can find almost everyone wearing the same brand of shoes." Mr. Sheppard, once again glinted. I felt my leg nudged.

"But that's because it's affordable! People in Oakridge doesn't care about which brand to buy but they choose the one with the best value." I need to take back what I said or else my boss will skin me alive.

"You see Mr. Sheppard, your products maybe cheaper because you don't need to pay for freight expenses but once we adjust our price to a very low price, it's only a matter of months before all of your store closes. So what's it gonna be?" And the floor is once again taken by Mr. Black.

"I'll think about it." with a sour face, Mr. Sheppard left the table and headed straight to the exit.

"I think that was a little bit harsh you know." I can't help feeling a little bit sympathetic with Mr. Sheppard.

"Yeah. Tell that to the guy who lied about his hometown." Mr. Black replied. He opened his wallet and placed a handful of money on the table before leaving. I had to follow him again.

"What do you mean lying? I am being honest!"

"Amplify is an established brand in Oakridge. You of all people should know that the locals are not fond of switching brands that are already tried and tested. It's true that they choose the brands with the best value but value is not always equivalent to price To them, they get the best value by buying Amplify products. But thanks to you, Amplify will now be owned by Black Industries. It's a shame it may never reach its full potential but nevertheless, it's a win for me."

"You bastard! You used me! I didn't know that!" That's it! Mr. Black is now officially the most vile businessman in the world.

"Maybe you do, Maybe you don't. But it's not actually your fault. That's how business works. Now, if you would just get in the car like a normal human being. I owe you a drink." he extended his arm and invited me inside the limousine. It's dark inside the car. Just perfect. I felt like I have sold my soul to the devil.

"And if I won't?"

"You're fired."

With a livid face, I went inside the car. Mr. Black soon followed closing the door to the limo. Damn him! A great manipulator.

"If you think I'm heartless then you really doesn't understand how the world works."

"How does it work? No matter how you try make a name for yourself, the rich will always beat you?"

"Don't beat yourself too much kiddo. The decision completely lies with him. I'm not forcing him to say yes. If he agrees to my terms then it's his fault." he opened the divider and said the next destination to the driver.

"Yeah. But I still think what you did was evil."

Mr. Black's expression changed like I insulted him. His face went grim and he was back again to his gloomy self.

"Tell me Flynn, never in your life, not even once, did you ever commit an act which you think are considered evil? I mean come on, we do evil things for the sake of our own benefits."

"No I don't." I replied almost in a whisper.

"Really?" he asked sarcatically.

I bowed my head and bit my lip to repress my emotions. Maybe I did something evil once. But that doesn't mean I don't regret what I did. He's right. Maybe I'm not that good of a person to judge what's evil or not.

"I thought so." he remarked with a sneer.

CHAPTER 6

Outside the Foreground bar you can find a long straight line of people. The music from within, together with the gleeful screaming of the people inside can be heard outside the facility.

Mr. Black walked confidently towards the entrance not minding the queue of people waiting for an opening. When the bouncer recognized him, the barricade was immediately opened. It's as if him entering the bar is a privilege to the establishment. I was also granted access when he said he's with me. It is my first time entering a first class club so it is quite amazing and flattering to be welcomed on this fine establishment.

The dancefloor is wide and even though a throng of people are in the club, you cannot feel that the place is crowded due to the vast area of the establishment. Mr. Black continued to walk until we reached another guarded section. The bouncer lifted the red barrier. The reserved area led to an elevator and Mr. Black brought out an electronic keycard which he tapped on the safety button. The door opened.

What kind of bar is this?

"Press the up button." he commanded. There was indeed an upward arrow on the mainswitch. Actually, the only choice is either up or down. I did what I was asked to and it was only a matter of second before the door opened.

And we're inside another bar. Only this time, it's more sophisticated than the one below and with lesser people. There was a dancefloor, a bartender, a counter, comfort rooms and other usual things you see in a club. There was a private lounge in a balcony just above the dancefloor, that's where Mr. Black decided to settle.

A waiter came to us and Mr. Black asked for a particular drink which I cannot pronounce or even understand what he just said. The waiter nodded and left.

This must be a separate club for the VIPs. I can see other people dressed in suits like Mr. Black and I kid you not, even celebrities are here!

There on the other side, a man is surrounded by a group of ladies while a couple is shamelessly kissing in the corner. I guess this is also a place where promiscuity and infidelity happens. A city version of Vegas.

The waiter came and placed a bottle of liquor and two glasses on the table. Once he poured on each glass he left our table.

"Have a drink. You deserved it." he lifted his glass like what you usually do to a toast. I took up mine and let our glasses create a sound.

I drank the liquid in one go and oh boy how I instantly regretted it. I started coughing as a response. I have drank alcohols in the past but damn, that's some strong shit!

"What the fuck is that?" I asked him.

"A drink." was his smart-mouthed reply.

"I think I burned my throat."

"Who said you need to drink it all at once?"

Whatever Sir. I kept my mouth shut and waited for the pain to subside.

It took me a few minutes before I finally composed myself.

"So what do you think would be the decision of Mr. Sheppard?" I started to make a conversation because I feel like I am having a drink with a cadaver who keeps on staring at me.

"He'll convince me to buy his company instead." he said."And would you like that?""Of course. That was the plan."

So all this time that was just a ploy to buy Mr. Shepard's company. What a conniving little shit.

I am starting to get used to the taste of the drink and it's actually pretty good if you take a sip once in a while. Strong but soothing.

I gave up trying to have a conversation with my boss. With his laconic and terse reply, who the hell would like to talk to this guy. Let him stare at me or whatever. I totally don't care. Also, I can feel effect of the alcohol eroding my body. I'm starting to get sleepy

"Ohohoho! Am I seeing what I'm seeing?" a loud voice somewhat got me back to reality. Hector came into our table and inserted himself between Mr. Black and I. He was a little bit tipsy, you can smell the alcohol in his breath.

"It's been ages since I saw you here! Did Madison finally gave you the permission to roam free?" Mr. Black did not respond so Hector turned his attention to me.

"You're drinking buddies with Magnus. Are you besties now?"

I also did not say a word because I didn't know what to say.

"Am I talking to rocks? Helloooo? Anybody?"

"Shut the fuck up Hector." Mr. Black interrupted. Hector smiled broadly and clapped.

"Finally! A talking human being! So tell me how's life?" After Mr. Black kept his silence, he turned to me again.

"We just met yesterday... Sir?" Funny how alcohol can make a person weird.

"Ah yes! The first ever male secretary of Magnus. You said my name sounds like a famous pornstar."

I sink myself lower in embarrassment. Mr. Black is here. He just apprehended me this morning.

"Ahhh. Don't hide yourself. Magnus said that to me first. Right Black?" Hector said in an assuring way. I leaned forward and looked at Mr. Black. He was so angry this morning about my remark and yet he said it first. Well I get that they're friends but you know, it must be somewhat true because he thought about it first.

"You must be a damn good assistant because Mr. Black invited you for a drink. Maybe I should hire you myself?" Mr. Mason commented. To say that I am flattered is an understatement, you can say that my ass is laughing with glee. I never received a single compliment from Mr. Black.

"Send your resume to my company and I'll directly hire you. You know-- ow!" Hector stopped speaking and massaged his left arm. "Now I finally got your attention!" he said to Mr. Black

"Try stealing my employees and I'll bankrupt your company." Mr. Black threatened dryly.

"Why are you always so heartless? You know, my cousin is not like this before he was-"

"Get the hell out of here Hector!" Mr. Black finally raised his voice. It seems like he's now really annoyed.

"Alright. Alright. Fine! Sheesh. You're like a girl on menstruation." Hector left us and joined his friends nearby. Thanks to Mr. Black it became silent again. We drank in solitude until the bottle became empty. Mr. Black left a wad of cash on the table and I knew it's time to leave.

When I tried to stand, the floor seemed to have twisted. I didn't anticipate the drink to have this much effect on me. The sudden dizziness caused me to grab for support and the nearest support that I could grab is Mr. Black. Fuck!

Mr. Black is not as drunk as I am because we did not fell together. It actually feels like I leaned on a wall because of his hard body. He helped me support myself and ordered me to move forward.

Somehow I didn't feel embarrassed about what happened. The alcohol must have reached my brain. Every step I take and my vision starts to swirl. As we went down the lounge, I saw people dancing on the floor. The loud music tempting me. I am not fond of dancing myself but tonight I seem to have lost inhibitions and care of the world.

"Let's dance." I involuntary muttered. Mr. Black looked behind his back to look at me. His forehead crinkled.

"Never mind." I didn't know why I sounded disappointed saying that. I'm not even a dancer.

"No. Let's go." he gestured me to lead the way going to dancefloor which I gladly did. I started to move my body in tune with the music. I don't usually dance so I just imitated the moves of other people on the dancefloor. Every movement I made feels like I am free. Free from everything. Work. Pressure. Bills. The past. Every-thing. It's just me and the dancefloor. But then I saw Mr. Black staring at me so serious and suddenly I felt self-conscious on what I'm doing.

"Let's just go." I said.

"No. You're having fun." He replied.

"I don't want to be the only one dancing."

And so we went back to the car. I feel warm, and sweaty, and dizzy. I also feel like I'm gonna puke so I closed my eyes before the car could even move forward. This was the first time in years that I felt so drunk.

There was a car crash.

A red car badly damaged. A tree cut off.

This is where it all started. A drunk driver being careless about any consequences.

Whispers.

I can hear whispers.

I tried finding the source of the sound and I saw my 17 year old self standing on the grassy field of Carmona Rosa. And as I went closer, I can finally hear what he's saying.

"Murderer."

I opened my eyes once I realized that I'm dreaming again. The pesky dreams are back again. Everytime I drink or my emotions are heightened, the past comes back and haunts me in my dreams.

I am still in the limousine with Mr. Black. I currently don't know where we are right now.

"Bad dreams?" he asked me in a way that I don't know if he's concerned or just would like to confirm if he was right.

"Yeah." I wiped the sweat from my forehead using my sleeve. My clothes are almost wet with sweat.

I opened the window to my side to cool myself down. In a few moments the car stopped in front of a fancy looking apartment building.

"You can sleep here if you want. You look tired and you didn't mentioned to us where you lived."

I'm literally dumbfounded. Mr. Black is offering me to sleep in his apartment. Is this concern or an elaborate plan for something else? I don't really trust him. He is after all my cold-hearted boss.

"Come on. I don't want to hear the word no."

I reluctantly went out of the car because he sounded irritated and impatient. The car finally sped off. I'm not sure if my apartment is nearby so I might as well take his offer to sleep in his apartment. I am awfully tired to make a wise decision right now.

It's not my first time seeing a luxurious looking facilities but every trip with Mr. Black is making me feel poorer and broke.

Apparently Mr. Black lives in the Penthouse. How obviously cliché for a wealthy man like Mr. Black. Everything is a show of power. They always like to be on top.

His apartment is wide and just like him, no personality can be seen. It's very minimalistic, the colors you can see is just black and white.

I found a sofa large enough for me to sleep so I suggested to Mr. Black that I will be sleeping there.

"I have another room there." he objected.

"No sir. It's okay. I'm fine sleeping here." before he could even object to what I said, I laid myself on the couch.

"Fine. It's your decision."

"Good night Mr. Black." I said before closing my eyes. I heard his footsteps getting away. I didn't expect him to reply but then he stopped walking. It must be the alcohol that I drank but before my vision turned dark, I heard a faint voice that said:

"Good night."

Chapter 7

The sound of the kitchen utensils woke me up. A blanket was wrapped over me but I don't remember going to sleep with a blanket. The last thing I remember is saying good night to Mr. Black. It's either he has a bit of concern for me or I got the blanket somewhere without me remembering it. I strongly believe it was the second one. Sometimes I wake up in the morning and the lights are on. I sometimes do things in the middle of the night without me remembering the act that I did.

Speaking of remembering things, I recall doing embarassing things last night. Falling on Mr. Black's arms, dancing foolishly in front of Mr. Black and lastly, accepting his invitation to sleep in his apartment. I would never do that. Not if I'm sober. Now I have to face him before work. And where would I change my clothes and take a shower?

And now I have to pee. I explored my eyes on the wide apartment but I can't seem to locate where the bathroom is. There's just too many doors! Now I have to face the inevitable. I have to ask Mr. Black.

I stood up and fixed the blanket before putting it on top of the sofa. I followed where the sounds come from until I reached the kitchen. Mr. Black is currently busy cooking and his back is facing me.

Uhmm. How can I interrupt him? My bladder's gonna explode soon.

"Ahhh. Sir," I said in a timid voice but he didn't hear what I said. I was about to call his attention again when I suddenly have the urge to sneeze.

"Achoo!" This time it caught his attention. He turned around to see where that horrible sound originated.

"Sir, I would like to—" oh god here it goes again. "Achoo!"

"Bless you." He said dryly.

"Sir, I would like to—" I can feel another one coming. I waited but then nothing happened.

"Yes? You would like to?"

"I would like to ask if I may use your bathroom, sir."

"Yes. You may." I waited for him to tell me where the toilet is located but he faithfully answered my question. Now I'm facing his back again.

"Uhm. Where is it located sir?"

"First door to your left."

"Thank you sir."

I went to my left and found the door to the bathroom. I took a second look inside before entering because it doesn't look like a bathroom. His toilet looks better than my room. After doing my business, I decided to snoop inside his bathroom. I'm not a creep or anything but I just wanted to know more about my robot boss.

What brand of shampoo does he use etcetera etcetera? And mainly because I am so bored.

I found nothing.

Literally nothing. That guy is the real creep here. The shampoo is placed inside a gray dispenser. The hand wash is the same. And you can't even distinguish the smell, it smells plain. Not the usual scent you buy like oranges, citrus, or any other fruit in the world. Obviously this is not his main bathroom but I wonder if I can see at least just a bit of human side of his. Maybe I'll find a brandless shaving kit, a nameless soap, an unnamed hair products. Jesus. How uptight is this guy?

I was about to wash my face when I saw a trail of dried saliva on my mouth down to my chin. Fuck! So that's why Mr. Black was looking at me with an odd look in his face. I wonder if I left evidence on his couch pillow? I really hate myself right now.

I washed my face and tried to freshen up even though I will still look like shit. Then I went out of the bathroom before he would even question the length of time I spent in his lavatory. A man who spends a lot of time in the bathroom is questionable if you know what I mean. I went back to the kitchen to say goodbye but he's no longer there.

And then I remembered, what if he is some kind of psycho and this is just a bait to kill me? Then Fuck! I remembered when Lana Winters was trapped in Dr. Threadstone house. That shit was creepy af.

"There you are." I almost jumped when I heard a rough voice behind me. I tried to act normal as if I was never rattled by his presence.

"Yes sir. I will be going now."

"I prepared a breakfast for two. You should eat here then we'll go to the office together." That sounds more like a command and not a suggestion.

"Thank you for the offer sir but I also need to take a shower and change my clothes." I reasoned out.

"You can borrow some of my clothes." He replied sounding aggravated. He really can't take no as an answer.

"But we're not the same size sir. You're taller and..." Bigger? How can I say this? "More muscular..." I'd like to say brawny but thay sounds extreme.

And he's back again with his silence. I am starting to realize that he does that to indimidate a person. Of course who wouldn't be intimidated to him? That's his special talen. Now, he's waiting for me to agree or make compromise that would make him happy.

"Okay. I'll stay here for breakfast but I'm gonna go home and change." I finally said as a last resort.

"Okay." His reply tends to be really laconic at all times. You really can't point if he's angry or not because of his aloofness.

He led me to the dining area where a breakfast have been served. We sat and started to eat what he had prepared. It was the usual thing you eat for breakfast. Bacon, eggs bread and some vegetables. I can't concentrate eating because we're facing each other and everytime he glances at me I can't help but feel conscious about everything. Am I chewing too loud? Does my mouth look big if I open my mouth to swallow the food? Am I eating too fast?

It is this time that I realized that he was wearing a plain white shirt, not the usual suit and tie that I always see during the day. He looks so normal that I can see his strong jaw being emphasized everytime he chews his food, the five o'clock shadow of his beard which complements his jawline that makes him look so ruggedly handsome. It's not surprising that he was offered to become an actor and a model because right now, looking at him feels like I'm watching a commercial.

"Take a picture. It lasts longer." I bowed my head in embarrassment. I didn't know I stared at him for too long.

At last we're done. That took a lot longer than I thought. Now I don't know what to do. Do I need to wash our dishes? Because you know, he prepared everything and he is after all my boss. I think it's unnatural to let my boss wash the dishes that we used. Gah! Stop overthinking Mike! He invited you to eat. You declined. He insisted. Period! Just get the hell out of the devil's lair and go home. But then what if this is just a test? Is he trying to see if I have the initiative to wash the dishes? Then I think I have to...

"Thank you for the food and accommodation sir. I'll see you soon." Was what I said before standing. Shit. I chose the wrong path.

Once I turned my back to him I cringed so hard at my decision. What was that? Mr. Black didn't say anything but I can feel his piercing stare behind my back. I contemplated whether to retract my decision or not but I finally reached the door to his apartment so I guess there's no turning back.

Last night and this morning is weird. I didn't expect Mr. Black to be welcoming, if that term is even applicable to him. I really think this is just a part of a bigger plan.

Be aware. Be aware.

Chapter 8

I just pressed the up button of the elevator and the door instantly opened. I stepped inside and was surprised to see Mr. Black. It seems like we're gonna go in the office at the same time.

"Good morning sir." I said but he didn't reply or even nod. It's the usual treatment we get from him. But why do I even bother? Just because I slept in his place doesn't mean he's getting friendlier.

Once the door to the elevator opened, I gave way so that he can get out of the elevator first. I watched his back as he waltz into his office. I can see coworkers acting at their best that I almost want to laugh. So this is what Mr. Black see first thing in the morning.

He entered into his office and I sat into my chair when the intercom buzzed.

"Mr. Flynn. Into my office now." Of course I obliged the boss' order and went into his office.

"Yes sir?"

"You're late." He said. I'm what? Does he have an amnesia or a mental problem? We just met at the elevator a while ago.

"But I'm not late sir." I defended myself.

"I didn't see you in your chair when I entered into my office. That means you're late."

Because I let you walk first you idiot!

I took a deep breath and calmed myself. I can do this. I can do this.

"We met at the elevator sir. Didn't you see me? I even greeted you." I faked smiled. This bastard doing some bastard things again.

"Yeah. But I'm talking about me entering the office first. That means I'm earlier than you."

Asdfghjkl! Bitch! Bitch! Bitch! I badly want to stab his eyes with my ballpen.

"Okay." I surrendered. I don't have the guts to argue with him right now.

"Okay." He replied.

"Okay." I replied back and turned towards the exit when he called my attention again.

"Aren't you forgetting something?"

Dammit it slipped from my mind.

"Your coffee sir." I bit my lip for my stupidity. Even though he didn't said a word, I can hear the voice of Walter White from Breaking Bad saying: you're goddamn right.

I sprinted my way to the coffee shop. This is the second time I forgot his goddamn coffee. Once I got into the building, I hurriedly went back to his office only to bump into Mr. Black when I opened the door.

Mr. Michael Flynn is officially dead at this very moment. He lived a very dull life.

"What the fuck?" He shouted in pain as he remove his coffee soaked tuxedo. The coffee is still hot and I knew for sure that

I scalded his skin. Lord have mercy! Who knoes what's gonna happend to me?

"I'm gonna get some ice." I immediately went to the office canteen and scoured some ice. The closest thing I got is a frozen canned soda. The company clinic is located at the first floor. It will take time to get there.

I returned to his office and I found him without his shirt on. I know that Mr. Black looks strong even when he's wrapped up in his suit but I didn't expect him to be this ripped. I think he should have been a model. He's looks like an exact replica of those classical sculptures. Every muscles are defined and aesthetically pleasing but what the heck, I'm here to alleviate his suffering.

I gave him the cold canned beverage. He furiously grabbed it from my hand and applied in on his abdomen. The affected area is now turning red. I stood there waiting for his next move or remark. I can already taste blood from biting the inside of my cheek.

"What the fuck were you thinking?" He asked exasperatedly.

"I'm sorry sir, I didn't mean to-" He threw his clothes on my face to shut me up. It's funny how the scent of his cologne and the coffee complements each other as they invade my nostrils.

"Buy me a new outfit. Any brand will do as long as its not cheap and ugly." He handed me his credit card and gave me no further instructions. I took the clothes with me and wasted no second to obey his order.

Once I got out of the office. Everybody was staring at me. They must have heard the wailing of devil and wants to know if I am fired or not.

"What are you looking at? Get back to work!" All this nosey business is starting to annoy me. I'm like their living bet.

Hey Michael, Are you fired?No. When will you be fired? I don't know. Why aren't you you fired yet?

See what I mean? Is doing a good job not a valid reason? I didn't go to college but I know I'm smart. I just let my stupidity take over sometimes. But you know, I'm still a damn good secretary. My reports are accurate, I don't forget important details and I always get the job done.

I saw a dry cleaning shop nearby so I decided to take his clothes there using my own expense. I don't wanna use his credit card cause it might reflect on his bank statement. After paying for the services, I went to closest luxury store to buy him new clothes.

It was this time that I realized I never knew what his size is. His garments must have been custom fitted since I didn't see a size specification on the inside of his shirt.

I was exploring clothes at the expensive corner of the store and the salesclerk is just eyeing at me like I entered the wrong store. Yes it's true that I can't afford this brand of clothes but my boss can and I need to buy him a new set of clothing as soon as possible. So yeah, I'm gonna need his assistance or whatever since I don't know what goes well with what. In the end, I just grabbed what I think will suit Mr. Black. I chose a white polo for at least a change. I always see him wear black except this morning when we ate breakfast together. White suits him. It makes him look less scary.

When the salesclerk saw me make my way to the cashier, he trotted himself to my side as if to assist me to the payment center. This bitch.

"I don't need your help." I said as loudly as I can. I already know his intentions. Every sale they administered will get them a commission or if they go beyond their sales quota, a bonus will be given to them. He frowned but he aborted his attempt to accompany me to the cashier.

The transaction was fast and I heaved a sigh of relief when the terminal accepted Mr. Black's card. I'm still a little bit unsure even though I know that his card can handle a large amount of sum.

I dropped by to the company clinic to get some ointment before going back to his office. I found him sitting on his chair busily typing, his biceps dancing with every movement of his fingers. He looks more intense and intimidating shirtless than in a suit. One wrong move and a punch will land on my face.

"I have the clothes now!" I raised my voice to get his attention.

"Good. Give it to me." He replied. His eyes still glued on the computer. I approached him and I can already see his reddish abdomen. I really scalded his skin big time.

"Here you go sir." I was expecting him to turn his attention to me but he just told me to leave the clothes on his table. I stared again on his florid skin. I can't just leave him in this condition.

I placed his newly purchased clothes on his table. I'm not actually sure whether I would really do this but I opened the ointment anyway, dipped my finger in it and started to spread it on the affected area. Mr. Black was startled with the sudden skin contact.

"What the fuck are you doing?" he asked. Annoyed but not angry.

"It will help soothe the burn sir." I suddenly regretted my decision but what's done is done. I need to push through with this no matter how ridiculously awkward this is . I continued to rub the cream on his belly. How does he find the time to go to the gym to achieve this kind of well-toned abs? I feel like I'm caressing a smooth rock.

"Are you gay?" he asked suddenly out of the blue.

"What?" Have I been staring to intently on his body?

"I mean do you like dick?" that's even worse.

"No sir. Why would I even-" I removed my finger on his body. I'm starting to realize that what I did is straight out of a porn foreplay. "I also got you some Tylenol. Drink that to lessen the pain. Your clothes are on your table and here's your card." I gave him his card and stepped away from him.

"If you will be needing anything I'll be right outside your office. Goodbye sir." I need to get away as possible.

"By the way Michael, you don't always have to call me Sir. It makes me feel old."

"I'm accustomed to call my superiors 'Sir'. Sometimes I can't stop myself from saying it."

"As your boss I encourage you to call me by my name. I'm not a knight to be called sir."

"Okay sir." he doesn't look pleased with my reply. "By the way sir, I'm not gay."

"Okay." he replied almost like a sarcasm.

"Really sir. I'm not."

"Sure. Whatever you say." he said still not convinced. I just let go of the matter. He is devilishly handsome and he knows it.

CHAPTER 9

I just got out of Mr. Black's office and I really, really wanted to scream and destroy some things or punch someone in the face.

Dicks!? The hell with dicks! I have one. Why would I want to have another one?

I went to the snack-room to calm myself. I'm gonna need that morning coffee now.

"Hey Michael!" Kate called me.

"What?" I almost shouted as an answer. She's gonna ask me if I'm fired or not.

"Nothing." She replied when she saw that I am not in the mood. "I just wanted to say you shouldn't worry. I'm starting to think that Mr. Black will have to be patient now in replacing his secretaries especially since the last incident." She commented and sipped from her mug. Okay fine. She wins. My interest is now piqued.

"Why? What happened?" I asked.

"Oh. You mean you don't know?"

"Just spill the beans before I'm gonna bludgeon someone to death."

"His last secretary Ms. Lorraine burned down his office. She was the perfect secretary Mr. Black ever had. Smart, kind, punctual and beautiful. You didn't expect it but man she was a crazy bitch. One night she went into his office and set the top floor on fire. She's actually the reason why Mr. Black has to move into our floor. I don't know what happened to that woman but we all hate her. She brought darkness into our floor and the reason why a lot of employees got fired." After her storytelling, she sipped from her cup of tea. Did she just...

"So you mean to say, Mr. Black is originally on the top floor?" No wonder...

"Yes. It's the executive office and the main conference hall. It's under renovation right now so expect in a few weeks that you will be transferred up where only you, Mr. Black, and loneliness will reside." Another loud sip from her tea.

"I'm sorry but why did his last secretary burned down his office?"

"I dunno. Maybe he fired her and she went cuckoo. That's why I'm telling you that Mr. Black may be a little bit nicer to you. He even hired a man to stop that from happening again." She went on to gossip about several things but I went into my passive state and heard nothing but blah blah blah. All I got is John is now officially the most hated guy in the office for microwaving a fish. When does this woman stop talking?

"Hey Mike, your telephone's ringing." Neil interrupted us, thanks be to God but once I realized that Mr. Black is calling, I left my coffee on the counter and ran back to my office.

"Yes sir, Do you need anything?" I said once I picked up the handset.

"To my office please." He sounded sour again. I wonder what I did wrong. I prepared myself again for another scolding or any other thing that might happen once I got into his office. I opened the door and I saw him standing in front of his table while his arms are crossed. Now it made him look twice as intimidating as before.

"Is something wrong sir?" I asked him.

"Notice anything wrong?" he replied back. I looked at him from head to foot. The only thing I noticed is that he looked… hotter? I mean he looked different since he was wearing a white shirt and not the black ones he usually wear. But overall he pretty much looks the same.

"A-" I was about to ask what's different but then I realized that would be stupidity. He then spread his arms when he got no reply from me.

"The clothes I bought are tight." I remarked when I perceived that his body is noticeably ripped.

"Uh-huh."

"In my defense, I didn't know your size."

"You could just ask me." After his rebuttal, not one of us spoke. It was just us and silence. And awkward eye-contact. What am I supposed to say? Is it too late now to say sorry?

"At least it makes you look more attractive." I said as a way to break the silence. A smirk formed on his lips. I already know what he's gonna say. And so I said, "No."

"You may leave." he finally let go of the matter and dismissed me. I thanked him and went out of his office. The nerve of that guy. I am in no way attracted to him. Him? Pfft. No thanks. I'd rather remain single for the rest of my life.

I went back to my table and not a minute later, I received an email from my boss.

From: MJBlack

For you reference:

Height: 6'1

Chest: 47'

Waist: 33'

and the list goes on...

What the f-, did he seriously sent me a copy of his body measurements? He even included his shoe size. Okay. So how do I reply to this? I typed: Received, with thanks. Even though I don't know how I would use that details in the future.

Now that I have composed myself, I continued on typing the minutes of the meeting and I have encoded at least an 8 pages when the computer decided to fuck my life and turned itself off. My work still not saved. I tried to turn the unit back on but nothing happened. I tried to do it again but still nothing happened. At this very moment, it's very hard to choose whether to fly into a rage or to stay calm and think of a solution. I chose the first one.

Some heads turned to my direction because the usually calm executive assistant is now spewing unimaginable curse words like never before. Abigail came to my aid and asked about the reason for my hysteria. I took a deep breath and pointed to my computer.

"You know you could just call the IT guy." she suggested. That sort of calmed me down. Why didn't I think of that? I thanked her for her suggestion and apologized for my wild behavior.

"Wait, how do I call the IT department?" I inquired.

"Just press 7." Once again I expressed my gratitude for her help.

I dialed 7 on the PBX. A friendly voice answered and I asked for some assistance for the recovery of my files. I do not trust the auto-save option of Microsoft plus what if the computer is permanently damaged. The person on the line said they will be sending someone to assist me. I said thanks and waited for that someone.

"Good morning, My name is Matt from IT Department. How may I help you?"

"Ah yes. My computer is not turning on and I'm also worried about my file not being saved." I replied.

"Good thing I'm also a certified Computer Technician so I can help you with both. Most people assume that IT people are also technicians but they do differ. Information Technology is a broad field." he interposed as he inspect my computer. "You're new here. What's your name?"

"I'm Michael by the way." I introduced myself.

"Nice to meet. You are the...?"

"I'm Mr. Black's executive assistant."

"Really? That's unusual."

"Yeah I know. I'm the first male secretary here and the like. I've heard it all before. It's not like it's a big deal."

"Oh it is a big deal. Trust me, I've been here for at least a reasonable time to know what's happening in the company."

"If you all say so. What's important is that I'm getting my pay-check."

"Alright! you really know your priorities. By the way, everything's now in order. You can resume whatever your doing a while ago." He rose from my seat and showed me the current file I'm working on. I didn't notice the time he troubleshooted my desktop. He is a great talker. You will really feel comfortable talking with him. I inspected the file and it's right where I stopped working

"Yay! Thank you so much for your help."

"You're welcome. If you ever you need anything, dial 7 and ask for Matt."

"Haha Sure. Sure." I reciprocated his smile and waved goodbye.

"Hope to see you soon!" He shouted before waving off.

"I don't think that's a good thing if I do need to call you!" I replied. I didn't know if he heard it since he's already out of my sight.

"Yeah, I don't think that's a good idea also." a voice said beside me. I was startled when I saw Mr. Black leaning on the marble desk of the reception area. How did he get here so fast? Totally unexpected that I got a mini heart attack.

"I-...Yes sir, how may I help you?" I asked him.

"Who was that?" he asked seemingly annoyed.

"That's Matt from the IT Department, he helped me fix the issue with my computer." Mr. Black is not as cheerful as I am.

"I tried calling you three times but you're not answering."

"I'm sorry. I didn't notice."

"That's because you're busy chatting with that guy." he cut me off before I could try and even explain my side.

"Sorry sir." was the only reply I could think of just to cut conversation. I can see that Mr. Black is not in the mood for some explanation and that he received a news that doesn't make him happy.

"Come with me and prepare yourself for some overtime." and I'm right again for the nth time.

CHAPTER 10

I followed Mr. Black until we reached the board room. Hundreds of stacked boxes are on the floor and there are still some men unloading from the utility dolly. What's happening?

"These are the books of our business portfolio. Others are still coming and now we need to arrange everything in order for tomorrow. My father is coming to inspect everything from every income and expenses." It sounds like he doesn't like his father that much for there is a hint of hatred in his voice.

"Why now?" I can't help but ask since it's now 3:00 in the afternoon and we need to sort through this mess for tomorrow.

"I don't know. Ask him. It's one of his surprise visit to know how well I'm doing in the business."

"Okay, What do I need to do?" I reviewed all the boxes in the room and there are different boxes labelled with different logos. How rich are the Blacks?

"I need you to review and sort every files from our different subsidiaries, make a summary of our top performers, the one we need to write off and did we have an increase of the net income comparing from the past year. If possible, review the year to date and month to date sales of Black Industries as a whole." The what? He said many things but all I understood was files. Damn. Even if I stay all night, I think we will not finish this tonight.

"Will anybody help us through these files?" The amount of papers in this room is really overwhelming.

"No one. These files are already audited but it's up to us to make the summary. Everything in this room are confidential but I trust you enough to gain access to our portfolio. Now start digging into these boxes instead of complaining." he handed me a box which he easily carried but it almost broke my back when I received it.

I started opening the box and some of them are just full of supporting documents of their financial statement so I just left them aside once I got all the information I need but some of them are just plain idiotically sent without an ending summary which makes you wonder why they sent it in the first place. I have to make their own summary even if I don't have a knowledge on how to do it but at least I tried. I even used Google for answers and took a crash course in business documents.

I look at Mr. Black, he's really serious about this matter. And I should too. I didn't noticed the time but I know that it's already evening since the sky is now dark. My head is starting to hurt from data overload but I really need to finish this for the meeting tomorrow.

"Here. You deserve a break." a coffee was placed beside me and I saw Mr. Black standing alongside my chair. He was holding another coffee in his hand.

"Thank you sir." I expressed my gratitude and took a sip from the coffee. I really am thankful to him because I do really need this. I cannot count how many coffee I have drank since this morning but all I know is that my body needed a caffeine in my system right now.

"Do you want me to bring you a snack?" Mr. Black asked me.

I stopped blowing on my coffee. Mr. Black is showing a bit of kindness right now. You know what's surprising? I think he is showing a real gesture of concern.

"No it's okay. I want to continue on my work as soon as possible." I replied.

"Am I working you too much?" he questioned me as he moved the chair beside me to sit on it. "It's okay to be honest."

"No sir. It's fine actually since I don't have much to do at my apartment besides watching TV or reading the newspaper."

"Your life sounds so boring. Don't you have anything to else to do besides those?" Of course he'll find it boring. Comparing to his likes and hobbies, I cannot do those.

"It's because I don't have the luxury yet to do what I want to do and I don't have that much friends in the city. Besides, I am unaware of the must visited place here. I only memorized a few route including the way to my apartment going here."

"What do you want to do?" he asked me and I stared into the distance because I was surprised by his question.

"Hmm. Maybe someday I would like to own my own house in the countryside. I would build my own garden and I would be there everyday to plant and do landscaping. On some days I would go to the river or the lake, do some fishing or swimming." I sighed when I remembered the old lake. I really do miss the mountains and serenity of the rural area.

"Even your long term plan sounds boring." he said arrogantly. I frowned at him because of his reply. "I was asking about your hobbies. If you have the money, where would you like to spend it?"

"A house? Wait, that's not a hobby. I guess I would go to the theater, or the arcade to waste some money. I can go to concerts of my favorite artists, try all the cuisines in all the restaurants in the city, buy all the clothes I want but I know cannot afford that type of luxury. It's okay to dream but sometimes it makes you unsatisfied with your life." I drank all the remaining coffee in my cup. All that somber talk made me aware that I am tired and sleepy.

"Let's continue the report so that we can go home early." I said as I put down the empty cup.

"You know if you're already tired you can leave all your finished works and you can go home and rest." Mr. Black recommended. I looked at Mr. Black to see if that was a threat but it's not. Is Mr. Black finally warming up to me or does he have a hidden kindness beneath his serious and intense demeanor?

"I can still work for a couple of hours." I replied even though my body wants me to go home.

"No. Go home. I can handle everything. You did a great job today." he patted my shoulder and I can't tell you how happy that made me feel. Suddenly, all the exhaustion and the weariness I feel was cleared from my body.

"If you say so sir, Thank you." I picked my jacket up and headed for the door. Before I went out of the conference room, I looked back again to Mr. Black. "Goodnight sir." I said and he looked back. I nodded for the last time and left the room.

I went out of the room with a smile on my face. This is a big thing. A milestone I have achieved. Mr. Black praised me for a good job. That's a rare thing. As I walk along the hallway, I saw Madison strutting her way towards me.

"Where's Magnus?" she asked me.

"In the conference room." I replied.

"Okay. Thank you." I noticed that she was wearing an alluring and provocative cocktail dress. I shook my head as she make her way to the boardroom. I bet she can't bother Mr. Black today even if she wanted to have dinner or attend a party. He is damn busy for tonight but why do I even care?

I looked at the digital clock on my computer, it's already 10:00 in the evening and we're the only persons left in the building except for the cleaners and the guard. I arranged all my things before I go and checked my table for pending documents. Satisfied that I have organized everything in order, I turned off my desk light and marched my way to the elevator.

The office looks peaceful and creepy at the same time now that every desk is unoccupied and empty. I got a feeling that I forgot something so I searched into my pockets for double-checking until I realized that I forgot my phone in the boardroom. I darted my way back and opened the door only to found Madison sitting on Mr. Blacks lap while they share a passionate kiss. Madison didn't see me because I was facing her back and she was fervently impassioned by the kiss but Mr. Black stared at me for my sudden interruption.

Strike three!

I closed the door and ran for my life. Shit! Shit! Shit! Did I just interrupted them in their private time? Are they doing something more than kissing? I don't wanna know. I pressed the button of the elevator repeatedly and cursed it for the slow response. Three floors to go until it reach my floor. Two floors. One.

"Where do you think you're going?" and I felt my soul left my body. Mr. Black is suddenly beside me. The elevator opened and Mr. Black harshly pulled my arm and cornered me with his brawny arms. I noticed that his shirt is not buttoned properly and his belt unbuckled.

"I'm sorry. I left my phone on the chair. I didn't mean to interrupt you." If I saw a new side of Mr. Black a while ago, now I see the usual seriousness but very elevated. I can feel the intensity from his eyes, a profound and deep hatred reflected in them.

"Why do you always have to say I'm sorry?" he growled. Why do I feel like his aversion is not entirely related to what happened a while ago.

"You can always go back and continue what your doing. I'll just get my phone tomorrow. I don't care about what you're doing. I saw nothing."

"That's not what I wanted to hear!" he slammed his hands hardly on the concrete wall and it echoed with the sound of his voice. I can feel my legs trembling. I've never saw him this angry. I did a lot of mistakes for this day. It's understandable.

"What do you want to hear?" was the words my mouth can afford. Does he want me to say 'I quit'? To give up my job? Instead he decided to answer me with silence. Our eyes doing the conversation, waiting for each of us to do something. I can feel my whole existence being absorbed into his stare, his cruel glare drilling a hole into my very being.

My breathing stopped when I saw his face getting closer, as if inspecting for an answer. I can feel the warmth of his breath and smell the scent of coffee from a while ago.

"Magnus..." Madison called him. He closed his eyes and sighed before slowly removing his hands from the wall, letting it slide in defeat.

"Just go." he said with a gruff voice.

I tried my best to compose myself and pressed the button behind my back. I heard the opening of the elevator and so I slowly stepped back struggling to get inside the elevator. Once I was inside the conveyor, I pressed the ground floor button until the gap erased their figures from my sight.

I know it may sound absurd and far fetched, but why do I feel like Mr. Black wanted to kiss me before Madison came to us. I shook the thought from my mind. Why would he? I interrupted them, not the other way around.

CHAPTER 11

The blinding light and the blistering heat of the sun made us seek shelter in the canopy of the conifer tree. Its thick leaves dancing along the light summer breeze. I looked at Hector standing beside me looking happy and at ease.

"You're car is now repaired." I said, a hint of sadness can be heard even though I tried my best to hide it. He's been with us for a couple of weeks and I know for sure he's gonna leave soon. Now that I'm used to his presence, I can't help but wonder what it would feel like being the youngest kid in the neighborhood. All of the people living here are mostly middle aged or retiring people. He was the closest to my age group. Yeah, he was 22, five years older than me but he was my only friend this summer break and I don't know what to do for the remaining days before school starts again.

"I like it here. It's been fun." he said and smiled radiantly.

"So when are you planning to leave?" I asked as I play with the pebbles on the ground with my foot.

"I don't know yet.I'm not yet ready to come back." his tone suddenly changed. Whatever his problem is he never bother to share. Since I respected his privacy, I never attempted to ask what was wrong. If he would like to share it, he can. If he don't, it's okay.

He smiled when he noticed that his sadness is showing. I knew it was an attempt to convince me that I should not be worried about something.

"Can I ask you something?"

"Yeah sure. What is it?" I replied.

"Do-" before he could even finish his question, I was woken up by my alarm clock. I grumpily switched off my buzzing clock. I tried my best to stood up immediately before I could even drift off back to sleep. Today is the day Mr. Black, the father of Magnus, will visit the office for the board meeting.

I decided to brush off the dream I was having since I can't see the relevance of remembering the past which seems so blurry now. I'm not even sure if what I had dreamed happened in the past or not but I do remember talking to Hector before he left Carmona Rosa. My recollections of the past are vague now. I can't even remember what his face looked like. Every time I wake up, the faces I saw in my dream immediately melts away in my memories. Whatever reason for reminiscing the past, I decided not to think about it that much. I have much important things to do.

I went into the conference room early so that I can get the phone I left last night. It seems like all of the boxes yesterday vanished without a trace. And my phone can't also be found. Am I in the right room? I went back to my office but I cannot find my desk. What the heck is happening?

I saw talkative Kate walking around the workplace doing her usual thing of gossiping with her workmates. I decided to ask her about my concern.

"Hey Kate! Where's my desk?" I'm starting to get nervous because I might have been fired but I wasn't informed.

"Why are you still here?" she asked me.

"Oh god. Am I fired?"

"I mean, why are you still here? The top floor is now opened for business. It's about time Mr. Black returned to his lair." she said. So that's why she's around here frolicking in the office.

"How do I get there? The elevator stops here?"

"Do you know the lone elevator on the right side of the building with a sign that said keep off?"

"Yeah. Why?" I asked when I remember what she's talking about. I always thought that that elevator was under maintenance or it's a building hazard.

"That's the elevator leading to Mr. Black's office. Only you and special visitors can access the elevator. You can get your electronic key card pass at the front office at the lobby. Aren't you informed about it? They usually send a text message or something."

That's the problem. I left my phone at the conference room but someone got it. I said thanks and went down the lobby again. I went to the reception desk and asked for my 'key card' or something that Kate was talking about. They asked for my name and after showing my company ID, they gave me a thin key card with my name on it and was marked as employee.

Then I went to the elevator on the farthest side of the hallway. I imitated what Mr. Black did when we went to that high end bar since I never experienced using one. To my relief, it opened with an electronic voice that said welcome.

The inside of the elevator was more elegant and luxurious than the one that I have used since my first day. It also contained the buttons to all floors but this time, it has an additional lone button at the top of all numbers labeled as EO. I reckoned it stands for Executive Office. That's the button I pressed without even using a single brain cell for my decision.

The elevator opened and I thought I was transported into a different office. The design and fixtures looks new as hell and my eyes cannot believe that this is gonna be my office from now on... that is, if I'm not yet fired. It looks refreshing to me since there was a whole lot of space for movement.

I walked straight ahead until I reached what looks to be the reception area. A PC was there with all my things in the table. A note was left on the desk which said: Board meeting. 9 am, executive board room.

It's 5 minutes before 9 so I still have time to find the executive board room. Kate mentioned yesterday that the top floor contains the office of Mr. Black and the main conference hall. I scanned the area and saw an opaque glass room and a door so I reckon that must be it. I opened the door and I saw Mr Black sitting so seriously at one of the chairs.

"Good morning Sir." I greeted. I still feel awkward from what I witnessed last night. He nodded and he extended his arm with my phone in his hand. I took the phone and said my gratitude. How come he slept so little last night yet he still looks fine while I look like shit from the lack of sleep? I sat on the secretary chair not far from the table. I wanted to ask if he had a good time last night but he might tell me to shut the fuck up or mind my own business so I just kept my mouth shut.

"Did you bring the minutes from the last board meeting?" he asked me.

"Uhhhmm." What would I answer? I was not present during the last board meeting so I don't have a clue who took the minutes. "No, sir. I only have brought the company record and books." Plus I'm not sure if the corporate secretary would be the one in charge of it or me.

"Then what are you doing? Get it now."

I stood up and went to my PC to check on the cloud storage if there was a saved record of the last board meeting which I don't even have a clue about. Nothing. I tried searching for keyword but there was no scanned copy of the minutes. If I am lucky it will be in the file storage area of the company but it might have a small chance that it is still there since majority of the files are stored offsite.

I tried looking at the active files but not a trace of the minutes can be found so I decided to try my luck on the restricted area of the library. I input my code on the lock and I heard a beep before telling me to insert my ID. I inserted my ID on the lock and this time it asked for my fingerprint. I did all of these and the door opened. I didn't know I can access this part of the building.

I inspected all the folders and binders in the room until I found a document dated last January. I scanned the document before returning it to its original place and I made my way back to the board room.

"Can the number of people present here constitute a quorum?" a middle aged man asked when I entered the room. Fuck. I'm late. They are already calling for quorum. All heads turned towards me as I made my way to give the files to Mr. Black. Somebody was sitting on my chair so I didn't know where to place myself.

"Excuse me, who are you?" the man asked me. He got the same intensity as Mr. Black so I guess he must be his dad.

"I- um." I seemed to have lost my voice by the sudden question. He sounded angry and annoyed that I interrupted the meeting.

"He's my secretary." Mr. Black answered on my behalf.

"I'm sorry but you need to get out. Corporate officers are only allowed in this meeting." he said.

"Yes sir. I'll see myself out."

"No. You stay." Mr. Black said, I mean Magnus since there are two Mr. Black present in the room. I looked at him. So who will I need to obey?

"Magnus. There's no chair left for your secretary." his dad replied calmly but cunning. "Please leave." he asked me one more time. I started to walk away but then again Magnus raised his voice.

"I told you to stay Flynn!" Magnus yelled, his voice echoing in the whole room. Now the attention was brought back to me, and to Magnus, and to his dad. Everyone was waiting for the next move.

"In case you forgot, I'm still the chairman of this corporation. I'm still your superior." There really was an unspoken feud between the two. Not one of them wants to lose. "Besides, your assistant's got no problem not joining the meeting. Isn't that right kid?" He turned his attention to me, expecting for some answers.

I looked at Magnus because I'm not sure who to follow. Magnus or his dad? Magnus is my boss but his dad is his boss. I chose not to answer and hoped that something will happen soon.

"Sit beside me Flynn! Mr. Turner is going to be absent, as always." It's like an impulse but I sat beside Magnus, following his order. Now I feel like a dog. Following commands like stay and Sit.

"You really like to do it your way huh?" his dad remarked sarcastically.

"Of course. I learned from the best. Now let's start the meeting. We already have a quorum." As if the matter has now reach its conclusion, everyone opened their folder except for Bennett Black, yeah that's it! I now remember his name from the article I was reading.

"But why does he have to be here."

"He's my assistant. I need him."

"Okay" Mr. Bennett Black surrendered. "Just reminding you to tread lightly, son. You know what I mean." I looked at Mr. Black, his jaw was clenched. It might not be visible to the others but he was gripping the pen in his hands so tightly.

Chapter 12

The reason why Mr. Black dragged me into this meeting I didn't know. I don't have a freaking clue on what to do here. I have no voting power, the corporate secretary is taking the minutes of the meeting. I literally have nothing to do except maybe create my own version of the minutes and take some personal notes for Magnus Black's reference. The only problem is that, I never knew anyone's name here except for Magnus Black and Bennett Black. So you know, I did the most reasonable thing to do, give them all nicknames.

Fat businessman #1, Fat businessman #2, Mustache, Mr. Clean, Squidward, Loudmouth, Weird Beard, and so on...

At around 10:07, Squidward provided an update on the sales progress of the company which was questioned by Mr. Clean. Loudmouth decided to butt in and asked some questions regarding the CEO report which was finished like an hour ago. Fat businessman #1 reiterated some information stated earlier... [a doodle of lines]

What the fuck am I doing? I came into a resolution to stop what I'm doing and just listen to them talk about business and money.

After a couple hours of mind-numbing presentation of figures and numbers, the meeting was finally adjourned. Everyone went out of the office except for Magnus and I.

Mr. Black still looks gloomy. I noticed during the meeting that his father was constantly challenging his performance and probing every figures down to the last cent. I wonder what the deal with them is.

"I noticed you stopped listening at the middle of the meeting." Mr. Black stated casually. Thank god there's only one Mr. Black here so I can call him that.

"No. I listened to the report until the very end." Which was true. I never stopped listening to them talk about business and money. The only thing I stopped doing was to take down some notes.

"I want to see your notes."

"I'll give them to you after I have encoded them."

"Give me that!" without a warning, he snatched the pad from my hand.

"No!" I tried to get it back but it was already too late since he saw my scribbles and caricatures on the paper.

"What is this?" he asked angrily as he points to my doodles.

"It's a shorthand writing or stenography. Commonly used by the police, journalists and medical professionals." I said as an alibi.

"So what does this elongated tornado mean?" he points to one of my drawings.

"Oh. That's when your father questioned the high accounts receivables. After a brief discussion with the board. A timeframe of not more than 6 months must be the given to settle the receivables. Motion to settle receivables; seconded and passed." I replied trying as much to remember what I heard when I was an active listener. Mr. Black seemed satisfied with my answer that he decided to question the caricatures of them.

"Mr. Flynn. Why do you need to draw an ugly illustration of my associates?"

"I just decided to imitate courtroom sketches but I realized that I'm a bad artist." Fuck. I'm running out of things to say.

"At around 10:07, Squidward provided an update on the sales progress of the company which was questioned by Mr. Clean. Uhum." He read a sample paragraph from my decent accounts. "Weird Beard. Mr. Clean. Squidward. Fat businessman #1, Mustac he... Are you trying to be funny Flynn?" this took the cake because I saw him become red faced.

"I'm sorry. I didn't know everyone's names that's why I gave them a nickname!" I said as a defense.

Mr. Black threw the paper to my face as a response.

"Next time be professional. I'm paying you to become useful. And don't think of me like I know nothing. I've had enough shit for this day! As far as you're concerned I know how to read and write shorthand writing. What you did was draw random lines and ugly illustrations!" After his outburst, there was an ugly silence in the room.

I never dared to speak or apologize. I knew that would be like throwing gasoline into a fire. The only thing I did was to look into the floor and wait for something to happen.

"I'll be expecting a more business-like minutes at the end of the day." He asserted as a resolution for my behavior and went out of the conference room. I picked up the scattered papers on the floor before going to my new reception area.

Okay. I admit. What I did was wrong. Now it's time to get serious. The first thing I did was to know the members of the board by looking at the Articles of Incorporation of the company, their annual reports if some officers were removed or appointed and the past minutes of the meeting. Lastly the most painstaking task of them all is to cross-reference their identity with my mental picture of their faces by typing their names on the net and stalking whoever results has given me until I found the right person. With my research skills and analytical thinking, I could easily replace Sherlock Holmes. Just kidding.

The majority of data from the minutes was taken straight from my memory since I stopped taking notes halfway of the meeting. Bless myself from having a good memory. After printing the MOM, I decided to give Mr. Black a peace offering for my behavior so I went out and bought his favorite coffee.

I took a piece of post-it note and wrote a love letter before sticking it to the cup.

I apologize for my actions. I promise to be more professional.

Ps. You would look better if you smile.

I'm not sure if the postscript would annoy or insult him but I went with it anyway. I knocked three times before opening the door to his office even without his approval.

"Yes?" he asked. Curious about my unsolicited appearance.

"I want to give you something." I replied. I walked ahead and placed the minutes and the coffee with the note facing him on his table. After that, I went out without uttering another word. For the whole day, I never heard anything from Mr. Black. No compliment. No complaints. No commands. Nothing. I'm starting to think the coffee with a note is a bad idea.

Five o'clock came so I prepared my things and clocked out. Circumstance really hated me because the moment I stepped foot out of the building rain started pouring down as if they were waiting for my dismissal. I have no umbrella in my bag so I depended on the nearby bus stop for shelter.

The rain never stopped and even if I would like to take a taxi, every taxi that passes by are all occupied. Damn it. It's not just me who needed one. I have no other choice but to wait until the rain stops so that I can walk down to my station.

After an hour of waiting, I was elated when I saw a vacant taxi but was suddenly annoyed when a fancy car stopped in front of the bus stop and the taxi driver didn't saw me hail the cab. The car honked its horns. I looked behind me if I have a companion here who was waiting for his ride. I'm the only one here. The mirror went down and it was Mr. Black who was driving.

"Get in." he said. I have no other choice but to get in the car.

"Please fasten your seatbelt." He reminded me because the sensor for my seatbelt was blinking. I had a difficulty with the putting it because it keeps on getting stuck every time I pull.

"Don't pull it too hard!" he was getting impatient.

"I'm trying!"

"Give me that!" he took the seatbelt from my hand and gently pulled it down until I heard a click. I again smelled his manly cologne.

"Thanks." I said.

"Where do you live?" he asked me. I said my address. He nodded and started driving. The whole trip was silent so I just focused my attention on the windshield as the wiper continuously remove the raindrops on the surface. I found the sound of it oddly relaxing.

When I got bored I tried to look at Mr. Black who was seriously maneuver the steering wheel. This was the first time I saw him drive.

"What?" he asked when he noticed me staring at him.

"Where's your driver?"

"What are you implying?" he replied.

"Nothing. It's just that from all the trips we made, this is the first time I saw you driving this car." He didn't reply so I returned my attention to the wiper. He really doesn't talk that much.

At last we finally arrived in front of my apartment. I said my gratitude and went out of his car but before I could close the door, I was surprised when I heard his even and powerful voice.

"Do you really think I would look better if I smile?" he asked. And that time, I feel like a big meteorite fell into my head. Did I heard it right? Is he asking if he looks better if he smiled?

"Yeah. You do." Was my answer still dumbfounded over his question. It's unexpected from him to ask silly questions such as that.

"Okay." And a miracle happened. Today at exactly 6:34 of July 27, the most stoic and emotionless Mr. Magnus Black flashed his most genuine smile. "Thanks for the coffee."

"Uh. Okay." I replied in a daze and closed the door to his car. He drove off. I still can't process what transpired for the last minute. I mean what the fuck happened? Is the world ending? I still didn't move and I didn't care if my body's getting wet from the rain. Something's happening inside me that I can't describe but all I know is that... I'm in a trance.

Chapter 13

"Michael? Michael Flynn?" I just noticed that I was inside the building when someone called my name. A familiar girl was now standing in front of me. I still can't get over the fact that Mr. Black smiled and thanked me for bringing him coffee.

"It's me! Janice!" she introduced herself when she noticed that I was trying to remember her face. Oh yeah. Janice. Now I remember her. She used to be my seatmate in freshmen high school. She had gained a little weight and she looks like she needed some sleep. "I didn't know you live here..." I felt my phone vibrate and so I brought it out and I saw that I received a text message.

From: MJBlack

I'm sorry if I treated you like shit today.

By the way, good job with the MOM.

I almost wanted to jump with joy after reading the text. What in the world is happening? Why is Mr. Black suddenly becoming so nice?

"Is that okay?" Janice asked me. I just knew she was saying something while I was preoccupied with Mr. Black but my mind never absorbed what she just said. "Please Michael?" What's okay? What does she need? I was thinking of saying no but then I felt a little bit of pity because she really looked like a lot of things are going on with her life. Plus she really looks desperate.

"Uh. Okay?" I decided to agree to whatever she just said. I'm ashamed to admit that I was not listening to what she was saying.

"Oh my God. Thank you! Thank you! Oh you are a life saver." She hugged me with great joy before she went inside her unit. I have no clue why I made her day. I also didn't know she was my neighbor. Whatever I have agreed to I hope it's not trouble. What if I just sold my sold to the devil?

It's still early in the morning but I heard a loud knock from my door. I ignored it at first because I was not expecting a visitor but then it was followed by a continuous knock.

"Who is it?" I asked while I walked groggily to the door.

"It's me. Janice." Oh god. What does she need? I opened the door revealing herself... and a little kid beside her.

"Here's Alexander. I'll be back by six. Thank you so much for agreeing to babysit him even with a short notice." Oh. So that's what I agreed to last night. "I want you to behave baby. Love you." she said to his son before thanking me again. It's too late now to say no. She was so grateful and happy. I mean what am suppose to do? I'm not even a kid person. I don't know how to take care of them.

"So... did you have your breakfast?" I asked him once his mother left.

"Yes." he replied. Now what?

"Okay. Why don't you watch TV while I freshen myself up." I led him to one of my chair and turned the television on. I changed it to

Nickelodeon before heading to the shower. I need to think about my alternatives cause I can't bring him to work.

After changing into my usual attire, I went out of the room to have my breakfast. I see he changed the channel to Discovery Channel. Good for him.

"Hey Alex. Do you want some?" I offered my daily breakfast, which is cereal, to the kid.

"No thank you." he answered without taking his eyes off the TV. I finished eating and prepared all my things before calling the kid. I also cannot leave him here. What have I myself gotten into?

"Come on Alex. Let's go." he turned off the TV and immediately went to my side. What an obedient little child. He took my hand which took me by surprise and so for the whole trip, he was either clutching my hand or holding on to my pants.

"How old are you?" I asked him to form a friendly conversation.

"Six." he replied timidly.

"Don't you have class today?"

"It's Saturday." Oof. Fair point. Why didn't I think of that?

"So how's school?"

"S fine but Aaron's being mean."

"Oh. What's Aaron doing to you?"

"Not to me. He likes to get Elijah's lunch."

"That's not right. You should confront Aaron before he grows to become a thief." I'm not even sure if I'm doing it right cause the old lady in front of me is giving me a dirty look like I did something wrong. Cut me me some slack here cause I don't even have a clue how parenting works. Once we got off the subway, I decided to take him to the play center near my workplace.

"I'm sorry but you can't leave the child here for the whole day." the clerk said to me. I looked at Alexander who was calmly sitting on the bench. Now where will I take him on a short notice?

"Please. I'll pay you extra."

"I'm sorry sir but it's company policy." I glanced at my watch. It's near my work time and it seems like I have no other options but to bring him to the office. Eh. He looks like a behaved child anyway.

Bringing the kid to the office is not a good idea as I thought it would be. It attracted the attention of some workers.

"Is that your kid?" Kate asked me before we could even reach the elevator. Oh no. Among all people we met this woman.

"No." I denied but then I know she didn't hear what I said because her attention was now focused on the kid.

"What a cute cute little creature." she squealed as she started to pinch his cheeks.

"Hey stop that!" damn this woman. She really can't keep her hands to herself.

"Hey guys! Look what Michael brought with him!" Sure Kate. Call everybody's attention you attention seeking frump. I pressed the elevator before the other zombies would murder us but it's already too late since we are now surrounded.

"Awww. Michael, you look just like him." Amanda commented.

"He's not my-" the elevator opened and my noisy coworkers stopped talking before running away from us. The reason is so much obvious. Mr. Black is in the elevator. We stepped inside the conveyor and I greeted Mr. Black as usual.

"How old is he?" He asked. That's a first. Bringing a child sure is interesting for him to initiate a conversation.

"He's six." I replied casually.

"What's his name?" he's talking to me but he was facing the metallic door.

"Alexander."

"Hmm." He murmured ending the conversation. Is he not even curious why I have a child with me or is it normal to bring a kid in the workplace?

The door opened and I, which have learned my lesson during the last encounter, went out of the elevator first and ran ahead to my desk before Mr. Black could enter into his office. Not long after he went into his office I was called into the devil's lair.

"I didn't know you were married." he spouted as if being married was something revolting.

"But I'm not married." What difference does it make if I'm even married in the first place?

"But you have a kid! Who's the mother?" he sounded like I ruined his mood by giving him a bad news.

"He's not my son. He's my next door neighbor's son. And why do you say it like it's a bad thing to be married with kids?"

He crossed his arms and leaned back to his chair.

"Because, married people especially with kids cannot be my assistant. Being married? Maybe it's okay if your partner doesn't mind the overtime. Being married and with kids? That's a big no. You'll be juggling three different role at the same time- a husband, a father and my assistant. What I want is your undivided attention because I'm that type of person who doesn't like sharing. Do you understand what I'm saying here Flynn?" Sure he has a point but he made it sound like he's a selfish asshole.

"Okay. Point taken but what if I'm in a relationship?"

"Are you in a relationship with his mother?"

"No."

"With other people?"

"No."

"That's what I thought. The HR wouldn't hire you if that's the case."

Okay got it. If you want to be an executive assistant to Mr. Black, you should be single and miserable. Preferably a lady with a kick-ass body but not required. People with no friends and social life are also desired. I wonder if the HR factored that in when he hired me.

"So? Do you need anything else?" he questioned after ten seconds of silence.

"No sir." Is he not even gonna ask why I have the neighbor's kid is sitting in my desk right now?

"Then what are you doing? Just go." he waived his hand to dismiss me.

I found Alex watching videos from my computer when I got out of Mr. Black's office. Look at that. He already knows how to operate a computer at the age of six while I was eating dirt at our backyard when I was his age. I pulled another chair from the conference room so that I can have something to sit on. For the next hours, we watched have watched unboxing of toys, Minecraft, fun gardening ideas, Nyan Cat 10 hours and hydraulic press vs. iphone. Man Youtube is weird. I let him choose what videos to watch. I just interrupted him when a Fifty Shades of Grey trailer played due to autoplay and when he attempted to watch a video of Happy Tree Friends because the thumbnail was cute (believe me it's not a fun cartoons). I'm not gonna be the one to explain all about the birds and the bees or why those cartoon characters have a fragile bodies.

Then the time came when I needed to buy Mr. Black's coffee. After a half hour of exhaustive thinking, I decided to let my boss babysit the kid while I'm out there buying coffee. God knows what the kid's gonna see if I leave him alone with the weird world of Youtube.

"Sir..." I said when I knocked into his office. I don't even know if he can hear it since his table is so far away from the door but I still did it to notify my entrance because he doesn't want to be interrupted once in a while.

"Come in!" I heard him say. That's when I entered into his office.

"Uhmm..." I started.

"Uhhm? You're gonna say something stupid aren't you?" Damn. Am I that obvious?

"Never mind. I changed my mind." I'll just take the kid to the coffee shop with me.

"No. I want to hear what you want to say before you leave the room." he stopped what he's doing and faced me. Now I regret coming here. What was I thinking? "Come on. Spit it out." Mr. Black egged me and I cracked.

"Can you watch Alex while I go to the coffee shop to buy your coffee?" I was hoping for his reaction but all he did was blink while staring at me and all I heard was the rattling of the air conditioner. I knew this was a bad idea! He is my boss for heaven's sake.

"I'm just joking sir. I wanted to ask if you would like me to buy something else or just the usual?" I said to save myself from embarrassment.

"No. Just the usual. And yes, you can leave the kid here for a while."

"Really?" My face must be glowing with hope for humanity but then I realized I broke an unspoken rule with Mr. Black: Asking the obvious and letting him repeat what he just said. "I mean, certainly sir."

"Hey Alex. Mr. Black will guard you for a while. I want you to promise me to be in your best behavior cause he's my boss and he's sort of a..." Monster? a beast? an ass? "an uptight guy so please be good okay?" I don't want you to be traumatized for the rest of your life.

"Okay." it looks like he understood my warning and so he's now ready to face a talking robot.

"Alex, this is Mr. Black. Sir, this is Alex." I introduced them to each other to make it formal.

"Nice to meet you Mr. Black." Alex said as a greeting. My, my, what a polite little creature. In the future if I will be having children, I wanted them to be like him.

"Nice to meet you too Alex." Mr. Black returned the favor and it's not exactly what I expected it to be. Mr. Black is nice? I mean, he's not the usual intimidating guy he usually is. It's like a PG rating of himself to perfectly describe his demeanor right now.

"Okay. I'll leave you two here now." I went out of his office and for the whole trip to the coffee shop, I can't stop thinking how it looks like in there. Did Alex annoy Mr. Black? Is Alex crying right now because he saw the face of death? I walked a little faster to find out.

"...And that is how you know you're in love." it was the first thing I heard when I opened the door. Am I in the right room? I can see

Alex sitting in Mr. Black's lap in a father and son way. What the f is happening right now? Mr. Black discussing love to a six year old kid? The world is ending! I'll accept it if he's talking about love for power and other people's misery.

"Here's your coffee sir." I placed the drink to his table. How can I call the kid back if he's sitting comfortably in his new found father figure?

"You didn't bought anything for the kid?" Mr. Black asked.

"Am I supposed to buy something?" cause he might question me for the additional amount when I will reimburse the total cost of the goods.

"You should. The kid is bored." he lifted Alex and I though it was just to remove him from his legs but then he stood up. "We're going on a trip." he said.

"Really? Where?" Alex excitedly asked like he heard a big surprise from his parents.

"It's a surprise." Mr. Black replied ignoring the coffee on his table. I have no choice but to follow them. Are we going on a business trip or a legit journey to somewhere fun and exciting. If you would ask me before I would say a business trip but now I honestly don't know anymore. Alex was holding my boss' hand as we walked to the elevator until we reached the parking lot. I can see that he's getting attached to Mr. Black. Unbelievable. He's more comfortable with Mr. Black than with me.

We reached Mr. Black's car which is obviously a black sedan. I guided Alex to sit at the back and buckled his seatbelt. I sat beside him but once I closed the door Mr. Black decided to complain about my sitting arrangement.

"What are you doing?"

"What? Am I not invited?"

"I'm not your chauffeur. Get in front." he replied irritably.

"Fine." I went out of the car and sat beside Mr. Black. Satisfied, he started the car. I can't believe we are going for an unplanned trip. Yay, I guess?

Chapter 14

I've been to many boring trips with Mr. Black and the common denominator for them is the lack of music. He never turn on the radio or even connect his phone to the car stereo. But this time, when he noticed that the kid was getting bored, he decided to turn on the radio.

Look! A Ferris wheel!" I pointed on a Ferris wheel that can be viewed even from far away.

"Will we go there?" Alex asked excitedly. I also wanted to know if we're going there. I'll be damned if we are.

"Yes." Mr. Black answered. Mystery solved. We are going to an amusement park. Never in my life have I expected to see Mr. Black go into an amusement park. The lord of darkness in a fun place? That's absurd but here we are. Nothing is really impossible.

Mr. Black took care of the tickets while I watch Alex gape at the attractions. Alex is not a stubborn kid but he sure got a loud voice. His constant remarks about how amazing the place attracted the attention of people. It was not until we went on our first ride that I found out the reason why people kept staring at us a while ago.

"Aww. What a cute family. It's rare to see a gay couple with their kids here. It always gives me hope." the attendant said it with admiration and romantic excitement. "You're so lucky your husband is hot." he said as he points to Mr. Black. Now that I realized it, we indeed look like a family. Two well groomed guys in a suit plus a kid. It totally screams gay.

"I'm sorry to burst your bubble but we're not a family. We're not even a couple, he's my boss, and that's just my neighbor's kid."

"What? You're not?" disappointment is evident in his voice but it was soon overshadowed by hope. "Can you give me your boss' number?" he tried to engage me more into a conversation but I decided to join my boss and the kid because I am already holding the line.

"What took you so long?" he asked impatiently. Thank god he's back to his old self. That's the Mr. Black I knew. Angry. Annoyed. Impatient.

"Nothing." I said. Nothing that would interest him anyway.

"It took you forever before you could sit here."

"You know what they say; nothing lasts forever." I smiled mischievously to further annoy him. It was effective.

The whole ride was mundane for it was suited more for kids under 8 years old but it was fun nonetheless. It's just Mr. Black who had no reaction of any kind. I guess he was bored but I think he was just being himself or trying so hard so hide emotions. Alex wanted to try the carousel next so Mr. Black and I were left outside the barricade to watch him.

"Sir, If you would not mind me asking, what pushed you to bring Alex here?" I asked Mr. Black.

"The kid was bored. I had to take him somewhere."

"Yeah. But why?"

I speculated that he would refuse to answer my question but then he didn't.

"I just wanted to give him at least a memorable time in his life." he let out a sigh before expanding his answer. "I had a boring childhood. I don't want him to have the same." It seems like our stony CEO had an instant connection with the kid and he wanted to be a father-figure to the child.

"I didn't know you have a soft side for kids. You know, deep down into your dark soul there's kindness hiding there. I'm surprised I surpassed working for you for a month and you still didn't fire me yet."

"I did almost want to fire you, especially when I was disappoint-ed to see a man sitting on the secretary chair. Usually HR hires women but then I thought you're..."

I squinted at him. "I'm what?" would he dare say it.

"You're... less emotional... since you're a man." Is he being sar-castic right now? "I didn't fire you even if you have your lapses and mistakes once in a while because I know you're smart and you always find a way to solve a problem."

"Thank you sir. This is the first time I actually heard a compli-ment from you." I can't help but to smile widely but I didn't let him see that because I turned my head away from him and made it look like I am watching Alex on the carousel.

"That's because I like you." he added.

Excuse me what? My senses seemed to have stopped but my heartbeat is rapidly increasing.

"Among all my past secretaries, you're the one I like the most. You're not a shallow person and your concern towards me is a genuine one. To sum it all, you're not a suck up." Now I can finally close my gaping mouth. Phew. I thought he liked me in a romantic way. That would be a problem. I mean, why did I even assume that he would be interested in me right? I guess I was just surprised if he was indeed confessing to me because he was the straightest guy I ever met and the thought of him liking another guy is like having a glitch in the system.

"Now stop smiling like an idiot. This might be the last time I'm gonna praise you. You're still not safe from unemployment, take note of that." And there you go. To think that he's a changed man is a stretch. I saw the carousel stopped so I waved to Alex for our direction.

"I want to try that!" Alex screamed when he arrived as he points to the nearby attraction. He even has the nerve to pull the hem of my boss' jacket. He was pointing to the bumper cars station. It was this time that I realized that Alex is now the boss of the day because we are now lining up to the dodgems.

Children 8 years old and below must be accompanied by their parents, that is why Alex chose Mr. Black to be his guardian. I didn't took it badly since children or people in general, really does not like me. There was no need for me to join them since the car is limited to 2 people only but I also don't want to miss the fun so the heck with it. If I want to play, I'll play. I was enjoying driving near the borders since I don't want to be colliding with other bumper cars but here comes Mr. Black who intentionally crash their dodgems to me.

"More! More!" Alex cheered. No wonder they get along; they're both a sadistic human being. I returned the favor to them and maneuvered my ride towards them. It almost threw the three us out of the car if we have't got our seat-belts on but they mostly took the hit since their car was thrown off balance. Take that suckers! I was laughing hysterically as I avoid them for the whole time until the buzzer rang indicating that our time is up.

"That was fun." I said as we exit.

"Are you hungry?" he just asking Alex but we both nodded as a response. We went to the nearby food corner. Mr. Black chose a healthy snack- a waffle sandwich with fruits in between. I'm not complaining since he's the one paying but he could at least pick something rubbish just for once like that big-ass burger filled with fries, bacon, steak, calamari and dipped in so much cheese that could give you a diarrhea or ice cream! I wanna live dangerously! Even though nibbled on waffle and had lemonade for beverage, it's still delectable. It's free lunch for me so I have no right to complain.

We rode more to different attractions. Sometime all of us. Sometimes it's only Alex. But every fun day ends. It's sad but at least you'll have the memories. When we got to the parking lot, Alex stopped walking and we got to go back to him when we noticed he's no longer with us.

"Can you be my dad? Cause you're the best person I have ever met." he said to Mr. Black. Something about the way he said it evoked an inevitable surge of sympathy and emotions for the boy. It was obvious that he longs for the love of a father. Something that was deprived from him even at a young age. He didn't want this day to end because the time that he returns home, it will feel like all the magic and excitement you have experienced during the day will disappear and everything will feel dull and dreary like it used to be. I know that feeling.

Mr. Black crouched down to face the boy. "I'm sorry but I can't be your dad. You have your father and if he's no longer with you, someone else will come into your life who will love you greatly like his own son."

"But why can't it be you?" Alex hugged Mr. Black and cried into his shoulder. The sight of them is making me emotional and I felt a teardrop fell from my eye. Mr. Black comforted the kid until he calmed down and agreed to ride in the car.

Alex fell asleep instantly and the car was back to silence with me and Mr. Black in front.

"Do you see yourself as a dad in the future?" I asked him. He's nearing his 30s and he still hasn't proposed to any of his girlfriends.

"Of course." he answered. Maybe he'll be the strict type or the father that will be the reason why their children will rebel or something but seeing him earlier made me feel bad for judging him. "How about you?" he returned the question to me.

"Seriously... I" I took a glance at the back to see if Alex is doing fine. "I don't know. I never see myself as a father. Heck I'm not even good with kids." In fact, kids hates me or dislikes me even without me doing anything. Maybe there's something about me that disdain them.

"How about getting married?"

"Maybe. But at the later part of my life. I'm at the stage in my life where I need to focus more about myself now than thinking about what the future would look like. Not that I don't care about my future but I just have other important things to talk about, if you get what I mean."

"Yeah, I get you." he nodded. "You want to get married but you're not sure about having kids which is weird. If your partner wanted to have kids, what would you do then?"

"You know what, enough of this talk about the future and let me enjoy my youthfulness first." because seriously, I don't know how to answer them cause right now, the lack of savings in my bank account is making me asexual to save money.

"What's that suppose to mean? I'm old?" he asked as if I offended him. That's tricky. How should I answer that question.

"It's not like it's a bad thing to be old. Men age like fine wine so that's something I'm looking forward to. Maybe someday I'll have the charisma and improved looks that would attract women."

"So you're telling me that I'm a charismatic good-looking silver fox? Are you sure you don't have a crush on me?"

"Again, you're twisting my words. Your words. Not mine." but sure, he's a debonair billionaire who can sow his wild oats if he wants to.

Chapter 15

There is a heavily damaged car in front of me with the color of blood which contains a wounded man inside. I reached out to him to see if he's still alive and that's when he opened his eyes.

He's very much alive!

"You're dreaming again." Mr. Black said. It is the first thing that I heard when I woke up. Where are we? I looked behind the back seat and I saw Alex peacefully sleeping. Right. We went on a trip to the amusement park and I feel asleep during the trip back.

"What's with the bad dreams?"

"What made you say that?"

"It's not the first time that I saw you this restless." Right. I was dreaming again when we went to that bar.

"I don't know. It's been years when I had those nightmares. Can I open the window?" He gave granted request and the way the cold air touched my face has never felt so good before.

"Have you tried seeing a doctor?"

"You mean a psychiatrist? It's not that bad. I'm just having some flashbacks now. I don't know why." Plus I don't want to spend a hundred dollars an hour for some conversation. It's not like I dream everyday.

"Then why are you frightened with your flashbacks? Were you abused or something?"

"No. It's nothing like that at all. I just don't want to talk about it. Like an embarrassing moment in your life. Thank you for your concern anyway sir."

"I'm more concerned about having a deranged person as a secretary."

"Sure. Same thing."

After a few minutes more of silence and we arrived in front of my building. It is safe to assume that I no longer need to return to the office because: A. It's near the end of my shift and B. We're here. I went out of the car and carried Alex who's still lifeless from sleeping.

"Thank you sir. See you tomorrow." I said to him before I closed the door to the backseat. However just as I'm about to enter the building I heard him shout from a distance.

"What do you mean see you tomorrow? I'll wait for you."

Crap. I walked back to the car to speak with him.

"I thought..." You know what? I shouldn't bother. I can't argue with this guy.

"You though what?" he shot back.

"Nothing sir. Aren't you tired from driving?" Goodness me. I forgot he had a driver. "You know what, let me just drop him home then we'll go."

"Don't bother. I'll just move the meeting tomorrow. I've had enough trouble for today." then he closed the window. The end. Now I have a kid to return to his mother. Of course, Janice was thankful for the help and she apologized again for the short notice. She took Alex in my arms and I watched her carry her son into his bedroom. I wonder what it would feel like if I had a kid.

"We gotta go." Mr Black said. I grabbed my essentials and followed him into the elevator. We are going to a personal meeting with Mr. Mason tonight at the Foreground bar. I was told it was the meeting which was cancelled yesterday so it was rescheduled today.

"You're driving?" I asked when we got to the parking lot. The limo is not present today and usually when Mr. Black drinks or go to the bar, a driver is always waiting.

"Any objections? Do you want to do the driving."

"No, sir." I shook my head in disagreement. I don't even know how to drive a car.

"Then shut the hell up and take your seat." he started to car and off we went to the Foreground bar. Again, we were granted instant access on the entrance and we went straight to the VIP section of the bar. Mr. Black chose to sit on the farthest side of the mezzanine, his usual throne. I'm starting to think he has dominion on this area because it's always unoccupied when we visit here.

Mr. Black focused his attention to his phone and his eyebrows are furrowed as he types on the screen. For some reason Mr. Black is taking me to his trips more often rather than letting me stay on the office as his proxy.

Hector appears to be late for the meeting and Mr. Black ordered a drink to sip on something while he wait in annoyance. I only accepted his offer to drink when I too got bored of waiting for his friend.

His phone rang and he answered it immediately ,deviating from his usual practice of ignoring it for a while until he decides to answer it.

"Where the fuck are you?" he grumbled but then his expression changed when he realized it's not Mr. Mason who called. I heard a woman's voice on the other line. Mr. Black signaled me to go off somewhere where I can't hear their conversation. I went down the mezzanine and sat on the bar stool near the counter while I watch the people on the dance-floor.

"Are you with someone?" a man asked and sat beside me.

"My boss. He's on the mezzanine." I pointed up.

"In that case can I buy you a drink?"

"No, thank you. I already got one." I showed him the drink that's on my hand right now.

"What's your name?"

"Michael but people call me Mike." and Mr. Black calls me Flynn.

"I'm Ace. Nice to meet you." he raised his hand and I accepted his gesture to shake hands. Somehow a stranger talking to me made me uncomfortable because I don't have a clue why he's starting a conversation with me. I bet he's one of those MLM scammers. One cannot be this nice without a purpose.

"I need to go back. My boss might be looking for me. Nice meeting you too." I politely ended the conversation and was about to return up when he held my arm.

"Wait. Can I have your number?" he asked. I knew it.

"Why?"

"Because, I'd like to take you to dinner if you're interested." Uhm what now? I stared at him. I don't want to assume but...

"Are you asking me on a date?" "Yes." he replied as he bites his lip."Sorry. Not interested."

Even if he's a decent looking man, I'm not really into dating guys or people in general right now.

"I'm sorry. I thought you were gay. Well this is awkward, gotta go, bye." he left but I was pissed off with what he said. Great. Mr. Black is not the only person who thinks I'm gay. But why? Do I have the face or do I give off the aura? I drank the remaining liquid in my glass for an additional confidence because tonight, I'm gonna prove everyone wrong.

I inspected the area for my possible prospect until I finally spotted a woman standing near the dancefloor. This girl is drunk and definitely desperately waiting for someone to approach her. I smiled when I found the perfect target. I made my way toward her in my semi-asshole walk.

"Hey girl, wanna make-out?" I asked directly. No more sugar-coating and beating around the bush. If it's gonna happen then it will happen. The girl looked at me from head to foot. Come on now. I've had my fair share of people who had a crush on me and if I had the money and the luxurious style of Mr. Black, I'll be having my own harem of women right now. Kidding. That's an exaggeration. Women describe me as cute but not hot. That's the problem. Because of my soft features they somehow associate me with being gay.

"Okay." she said. That's my girl. I smiled and took her closer to me before kissing her. I never noticed how long we were exploring each other's lips but I never thought I would enjoy it to the point that we were caressing each other as the kiss gets deeper.

A loud crash was heard like a glass was broken. Some girls screamed in terror at the sound. Everyone stopped what they're doing for a second to find out what happened before resuming to their business when they saw it was just nothing. It's not nothing to me. I had a feeling it came from the mezzanine and I was right when I saw Mr. Black coming down from the stairs with a heavy foot. He looks pissed. Like really pissed. It must have something to do with the phonecall with his girlfriend.

"Let's go. Hector is not coming." he was really infuriated that he had to drag me out of the bar to the parking lot. I think I just discovered a new level of Mr. Black's anger scale.

"What happened?"

"Get in." he snarled like a mad dog.

"Are we going somewhere or are we done for the day? Cause you don't need to take me home. I can ride a taxi." he stared at me with ferocious aggressiveness. Somehow Mr. Black turned into some kind of beast for him to behave this feral. I sat on the passenger's seat and I was not prepared on what would follow after.

Mr. Black really stepped up the pedal to the metal because the car is going fast that it can the heavens. There's nothing I could really do except clench on the seatbelt for my dear life in case we crash into something. I looked at Mr. Black who was driving silently driving. His jawline was emphasized from gritting his teeth and his hands are tightly clamped on the steering wheel. I've never seen him this stiff and angry before. The accelerated speed of the car made me remember a scene from the past. The red car. The old breakfast and bed. The accident.

Finally, the car decreased in speed and halted to a stop. We're in front of my apartment building. I took a minute to calm myself

down. He's not saying anything, I can only hear his loud breathing
. His hands are still tightly bound on the wheel and you can see
the outline of his veins from too much pressure.

"Hey. Are you alright?" I placed my hand on his hand to try and
loosen his grip because I can see that something is really bothering him. He withdrew his hand while he hissed as if touching him
burns.

He stared at me. His lips opened and I expected him to say
something but he closed them back.

"If you're not talking then I hope you will feel better soon. Good
night Mr. Black. Thanks for the ride. See you tomorrow." I opened
the door and went out of the car.

"How many relationships have you had" he asked before I could
even close the door. I swung the door back to see him.

"What?"

"Just answer the damn question!" he screamed and I was stupefied by his sudden outburst. I gulped before answering.

"About three. Why?"

"Three. Unbelievable." he chuckled sarcastically. Did he drank too
much or is he losing his mind? "What would you do if someone
doesn't love you back?"

"I don't really have the credentials to answer that question." I
said. He laughed again before making a sneering comment.

"Of course. How can they not love someone like you."

Okay. I'm pissed. Now he's just being an asshole.

"I really think it's not fair that you insult me like that. You are
clearly the bigger man here. You're handsome, smart and rich.
Everybody will love you because you literally have everything.

You are the true definition of perfection. Now stop this sad shit delusion and go home you're just drunk."

"Do you love me?" he said. I seriously don't know how to answer that. "That's what I'm talking about. You're wrong. I am not perfect. People leave me when they can no longer endure me but they choose to stay because of money. I'm lucky you still have the guts to be my secretary. This time, when I was sure that I finally got someone who genuinely loves me, I found out I was wrong. That's what made me angry because I felt like a fool!" he grabbed the handle to my door and closed it himself with a loud thud before driving away.

CHAPTER 16

"Flynn! I need the copy of the Edison contract."

"Yes sir. Coming right up." I got the contract on the table and went inside his office. Mr. Black is seated silently on his chair as if he was waiting for me, both arms were folded across his chest.

"Please have a seat Flynn." he said. Whatever the matter is I think it's really serious. I sat down. Mr. Black stood up and circled his way around the table until he reached my side. He maneuvered the chair around for me to face him.

"I asked you if you love me."

"What's this all about?"

"Do you have feelings for me Michael?" he leaned forward putting both his hands on the armrest.

"Why are you asking me that?" I felt my voice quaver with every word. Somehow this is making me tremble. I can feel my heartbeat getting faster and faster.

"I know you want me." he whispered seductively to my ear sending shivers down my spine.

"I'm not gay!" I gathered all my strength left to scream at him so that maybe he can stop with whatever this is.

"You always say that." I tried to leave but he pushed me down to tame me. "But you'll never know if you always resist to what you are feeling." he gave a quick kiss to my lips and I felt my body go limp with mixed emotions. "Maybe it's time you give in to your desires." he murmured as softly as his lips.

I looked at him starting from his smoldering stare with his coffee colored eyes down to his succulent and parted lips. I can hear my own heartbeat amidst my nervous breaths. This is something that is against me but I reached up and pulled him closer to me until our lips met. We started kissing gently until it started to go deeper and demanding, pulling ourselves harder against each other. It is nothing like I've experienced before. I felt myself dissolving from this sin but I don't care. He groaned softly, a sound that makes me crave for more. Our arms started to explore each other , caressing every part, every skin there is to hold.

With his strong arms, he managed to carry me to the table to level us up. He started to unbutton my shirt and I did the same to him.

I was actually enjoying myself when consciousness took over me. I noticed the flaw of the scenario and the absurdity of what's happening. In just a second, reality obliterated what seems to be a sex dream and that's when I opened my eyes. I panted for some air and suddenly, I am back again in my room. Did I just dreamed about kissing my boss? The scary thing is that, I somehow liked it.

I let my fingers run into my lips. Everything seems real and stimulating.

I blame everyone for this. Ace. The girl at the club and Mr. Black. It's a combination of what transpired this evening and it went inside my head for some reason. If dreams are a product of our subconscious, then does that mean that I have the hots for my boss?

Eh. As if!

Sleep it of Michael. Be thankful it's not one of your bad dreams.

I take that back. It was a nightmare.

Somehow I still think about that dream and it's making me a little bit jittery while I wait for Mr. Black. I searched about dreaming of sleeping with your boss or doing with it the same sex and it assured me that there's nothing wrong about it because dreams are just symbolical and should not be taken literally. I mean, it's not even a sex dream because I woke up before I even get to know who stabbed who. Honestly, I don't want to know.

The elevator opened; revealing Mr. Black. Something changed. I don't know but there's something new about Mr. Black.

Sexual awakening.

A little voice whispered inside me. Pfft. I did not. I just woke up from an almost sex dream. It's not like I am sexually awakened. Mr. Black is definitely not a harbinger of my sexual awakening. It is Jessica Rabbit who woke me sexually. Because of my internal monologue, I never got the chance to greet him. It's a first but I think he didn't mind it.

The time came when I need to get him his usual coffee. When I gave him the coffee, my eyes focused on his table which its reputation is now forever tarnished together with the chair in front of it. It's worse than I thought when I shuddered when our fingers touched as I pass him the cup.

Gosh darn it! Did I turn into a woman because I feel like I have hormones acting up. For some reason, I didn't walk out of his office. I watched him sip from the coffee cup with my eyes focused on his lips as it makes contact with the lid. Somehow, I wondered how his lips would taste like in real life.

Am I seriously having an instant crush on Mr. Black because of an erotic dream? It's like the universe is telling me to explore my sexuality. It's not actually a taboo to try it since many people experiment with their sexuality in college and I didn't go into that phase because I never went to college. Just yesterday, I was scared of him and he looks like a normal human being but now I think he's so fine in his suit and I find his serious demeanor so attractive.

"Do you think it's time for me to finally try dating guys?" I blurted out. Mr. Black paused for a moment before he looked at me.

"What?"

"You think I'm gay. The guy at the bar thinks I'm gay. I think Matt from IT is hitting on me too. Maybe it's a sign to date other guys. What's the point of acting straight when most people thinks I'm not. Who know's, what if I'm actually bisexual?"

"That is absolutely the most rubbish thing I ever heard today. Don't piss me off today Flynn. I am not in the mood." he continued to sip from his coffee.

"Would you ever consider dating me?" The question took him by surprise and he spat his drink by spraying coffee all over his table. I'll take that as a no.

"Oh yeah. I'm sorry. You're in a relationship with Madison." I bit my lip at the realization of my stupidity. I am now sure this is the moment that I will be fired from my job. Mr. Black coughed the remaining liquid in his throat.

"Are you serious?" he asked me when he finally composed himself.

"No. I'm totally kidding." I tried to salvage whatever's left in my dignity.

"You sounded serious a while ago. Now, why would you like to take me on a date?" he clasped his hand together like he usually do when he interrogates a business partner.

He was staring at me searching for an answer and my mind panicked. In the end, I blurted out what my mind could come up with an excuse in a short span of time. "I don't want to share the details but I really find you attractive right now."

I think my mind was melted if you call that an excuse.

"Really? Why?" he asked with a mischievous smile plastered on his face.

Instead of replying, I guess I'll pack up my things and go. No need to embarrass myself any longer.

"I quit, sir." I said and headed for the exit. You are lame Michael, don't you know that?

"Request not granted. I need you to clear my afternoon schedule. I'm gonna take you to dinner tonight." he said. I stopped walking. Did I heard it right? He's taking me to dinner? Tonight? Is that an invitation to a date or a meeting?

I turned back. "What? Are you being serious?"

"Yes."

"Are we going on a meeting?"

"No."

"Then what's it about?" I inquired. I don't want to assume anything.

"You said it so yourself. A date."

"But what about Madison?" she's not gonna be happy knowing that her boyfriend is taking his secretary on a date.

"We broke up yesterday." he replied as he wipes the coffee droplets on his table. Is that the reason why he was so pissed yesterday?

"You know, you don't have to do this if you don't want to. It's not ideal to find a rebound a day after breaking up." besides, I'm not even sure I should be doing this. Dating a guy and exploring my sexuality by dating my boss.

"I'll take you on a date because I want to date you for real Michael Flynn."

Chapter 17

I could not believe I am actually doing this. This is wrong. I should not be doing this! But everything's settled. Mr. Black dismissed me early to prepare for our so called 'date'. I am now in my apartment dressed in perfection and trying to give myself a pep talk in front of a mirror. I'm gonna do this. I got myself way too deep to back out.

I closed my eyes to calm myself for the last time. If I'm gonna do this, I should be ready to face the past. I am aware that it will soon come back to haunt me and it will be more terrifying than before. I can already feel it. I'm scared.

"I'm sorry mother. I did my part." I whispered to myself as I take a last look on the mirror before turning the lights off. "Believe me I tried. I really did."

Just as I came out of the building, I saw Mr. Black standing beside a limousine with a bouquet of flowers in his hand. He looks sharp and handsome in his suit.

"Uhm. What is this?" I asked.

"A flower?" he replied plainly.

"No. I mean, this." I pointed at the limousine and the flower. "Why?"

"It's an established dating etiquette."

"Yes. But I'm not a girl."

"Don't you like it?" he muttered .

"Well, umm." I squirmed and looked down to avoid the intensity of his stare. "To be honest, I'm a little overwhelmed.."

I saw him tighten his grip on the bouquet.

"But I like it." I said. He smiled in relief and passed me the flowers. It contains two of my favorite flowers: pink carnation and red roses. The arrangement is marvelous, the red roses are sorted to form a heart shape which is surrounded by the pink carnations. "How did you know I favor these flowers?"

"You're from Carmona Rosa . I concluded it might remind you of home." He's good. He really did his research. Carmona Rosa is not only known for the red river but also for the flower plantation for roses, carnation, chrysanthemums, alstroemerias and others.

He assisted me inside the limousine and sat beside me which is a first time in a limo ride. He usually goes first and I sit in front of him as his assistant. I rubbed my hands together to distract myself from fainting.

"You know, this is my first time doing this." I broke the silence.

"Me too." he replied.

"I don't want people to see us together or even think that we're on a date until I figured myself out." I bit my lip nervously. It's me who had the guts to ask him on a date yet I'm the one who's unsure about going out.

"I know." he said. "That's why I arranged everything for you."

"You did? How did you know?"

"I can read people. I know that somewhere in your mind you're thinking about backing out." he smirked knowing that he did the right move.

"Where are you taking me?"

"To dinner." he said in a suave way. Looking at him so confident and cool about everything made me feel at ease. Peaceful. And That I should not worry about anything. But still I cannot think about any reason why he agreed to do this. I still can't shrug off the feeling that he's hiding something.

"Is this really necessary?" I asked when he gave a blindfold for me to cover my eyes.

"Yes." he replied. "It will spoil the fun if you see where we're going."

"Okay." I reluctantly put the blindfold over my eyes and I can finally see nothing but darkness. The car made several turns until it finally stopped. I was about to remove the blindfold but he warned me it advance.

"Don't remove it yet." I felt his warm hand stop mine. I gulped when his touch nearly made me gasp. "Now, I need you to follow me." he held my hand and assisted me out of the car. "Now, walk with me." he said.

Still holding my hand, I was taken to whatever direction he wanted us to go. His hand felt comfort and security as we walk along the way. It's a funny thing though, this is the only time our skin touched each other longer than ten seconds. It feels oddly invigorating. I want to giggle like a teenage girl.

I knew we rode an elevator so it's not a restaurant, a restaurant can't have this many floor. We walked on a stairs until I felt the air when we went out the door. A rooftop perhaps? Or a helipad because we're going to ride a helicopter.

Mr. Black removed the blindfold from my eyes and his face is the first thing I saw.

"Well. What do you think?" He stepped aside revealing a romantic dinner set-up on a rooftop complete with candle lights, flowers and lots and lots of rose petals. This is excessively romantic. A straight out of a romantic movie.

"Well?" What do I think about it?

"Do you want the truth?"

"Of course."

"It's too cheesy." he frowned upon hearing my answer. "But I kinda like it."

"What do you want?"

"I honestly don't know. You see, I'm new to this." he led me to the center where the table lies and helped me took a seat.

"The women usually squeals with joy for something like this. You however managed to cringe at the sight of this."

"But I'm not a woman. How did you even managed to arrange something like this in a day?"

He finally sat down. "I have my ways."

Money. Makes everything easier if you have it. It's feels different to be the one being surprised because I'm the one who usually plan when I go on a date. But it's nice too. A new perspective for me. Mr. Black really did an excellent job with this. It feels really romantic. A candle light dinner under the stars with a great view of the city.

"Can I ask you why you agreed to do this?"

"That 's an unusual dinner conversation." he said. "You sounded like you're doubting your date." he started to pour the wine on both of our glasses.

"I do. Why the sudden change of heart Magnus?" calling him by his first name took him by surprise.

"I could ask you the same question."

"Really, why?"

"Because I like you!" he lowered his gaze and started to tap on the table. It is the first time I've seen him this awkward and unsure. "I've always like you and when you asked me if I could date you,

"I mean how? Why this," I pointed to myself. "If you could be in a relationship with someone as hot a Maddison."

"You have the personality of a woman and I um" he stammered. "I have a thing for my secretaries." he saw that I was somewhat confused with his choice of words, that's why he stopped talking. "Your turn. Why did you asked me out."

I couldn't tell him the reason even if I wanted to. It's not just about the sexual dream, it's something that takes place even before I was employed at Black industries. Somewhere in the corner of my eyes I saw my mother shaking her head in disapproval.

"Let's eat before the food get cold." I tried to change the topic. He didn't press into the topic further and I'm grateful for that. There is something that I couldn't tell him.

"How's the food?" he suddenly asked.

"It's okay." I replied. I'm not really into steaks but it's in the serving. Somehow raw steak disgusts me, I feel like I'm eating uncooked meat and well-done is just too dry and difficult to chew and swallow. Medium rare to well done is still rare in my opinion.

I can't stop thinking about tapeworms and other parasites that is not killed in the process. If I see pink, it's under-cooked. Period.

"You don't. And that chef convinced me that you'll love it. He will be indemnified." I heard him grumble, his eyebrows furrowed.

"Easy there, tyrant. Look I liked the dish. Most of it so far but the point the chef did a good job. It's just that I prefer chicken compared to other types of meat."

"I'm sorry. I just want this to be perfect."

"For a starter, you're doing great! You're actually doing it too much for a trial version."

We continued eating until we got to the dessert which I really adore. It's the only course I loved among everything. The cake is so fluffy and tasted like heaven and the filling, my god the filling, words can't express how delectable it can be.

"What?" I asked. Mr. Black is staring at me with a perennial smile. I wiped my mouth in case some icing is left on my lip.

"You look cute." he replied.

"Stop patronizing me. It doesn't suit you." I don't care what anyone thinks but I'm not buying this saccharine Mr. Black. It's not in his nature to be this sickeningly sweet unless something's up.

"You never told me about your former secretary, Lorraine. What happened between the two of you? Why did she burn your office?" I remembered what Kate told me before. His last secretary burned down his old office but no one knows the reason. Kate mentioned that she was smart and kind until she turned into a crazy bitch.

"Who told you about her?" Mr. Black's tone went sour, confirming my hunch.

"I just heard it somewhere." I replied. I didn't want to snitch on Kate. As talkative and annoying she was, I don't want her to lose her job because of me. We stared at each other until he growled before he unwillingly told me the answer.

"I had a secretary before you. Her name's Lorraine. An efficient worker. A woman with beauty and brains." I listened intently for what he's about to say next. I already know that part of the story. "One night she tried to seduce me. I told her no. I thought that was it but it went on and on as a cat and mouse chase until she went ballistic. I saw her true colors, she was obsessed with me. I never realized how far it was until she decided to burn my office cause she thought I was inside. I lied to her about my location. She texted me asking where I was and I said I'm working on something urgent in my office but actually I was driving."

I could not believe it. He's texting while driving? Joking aside, something's not adding up to all of this, whatever this is that he's doing. He just told me he has a thing for his secretaries. Why decline the advances of her former secretary but agreed in an instant to my subtle invitation.

"Why didn't you date her.""She's not my type.""I'm confused.""I'm not."

Why did I fell like I feel into my own bait? He answered as fast as I released my statement. Did he prepare for it or he's actually telling the truth? I noticed him eyeing my lips. Did he really want to kiss me that night when I caught him with Maddison? I don't understand but I want to kiss him too.

I leaned forward. He did too.

In an instant, a drop of water fell on my nose only to be followed by a downpour of rain. We immediately stood up to find some shelter. I ran to my side to find the exit but Mr. Black held my hand, telling me that I'm going the wrong way and that I should follow him. I can see every candlelight perish from the excessive rainfall just as we entered into a room.

It was still dark but I noticed we're inside his apartment. He took me on a date on his penthouse all along. We looked at each other, wet from the rain and relieved from the rapid panic. I chuckled at the sight of us two. I stopped when I saw Mr. Black looking at me thoughtfully.

"What?"

"Damn. I want to kiss you right now." he said, his voiced filled with frustration.

I felt the world stop for a moment. My eyes focused on his plump red lips, waiting for my decision.

"Do it. Kiss me." I urged him. It's wrong but I want to taste it.

And then I felt it. His lips brushed softly against mine, softly and delicately like rain on a summer evening. I opened my mouth to welcome him fully and willingly participate into this sin of lust. I can feel my legs getting weak with each stroke, my body limp with desire. I grasp tightly to the sleeves of his jacket; never caring if the excessive crumpling of his suit hurts him. I need to take hold of him or else I'm gonna fall. Because if I fall, I'll hurt myself.

Chapter 18

The kiss started off soft until it went deeper and deeper. Mr. Black hungrily pushed me back into the wall, his lips aggressively moving as if he was trying to win a battle. I felt his tongue slid across my bottom lip making me shiver in excitement, the stubble of his beard scratching against my cheek and jaw. I've always loved that five o'clock shadow of his. It suits him: manly, rugged and a man with social maturity.

I've kissed and been kissed, but his kisses take me back to my first kiss, the feeling of euphoria with a rush of adrenaline that melts your body into oblivion. His hands started to unbutton my shirt. I did the same with him until his shirt is wide open. He took the liberty to take them off revealing his lean body hidden under those fabrics. I let my fingers run across his chest feeling his brawny muscles. He cupped my face back and continued to kiss me while I explore his body by touching every skin starting with his chest until I reached his abdomen, his arms, and eventually his back. A moan escaped from my lips when he started kissing my neck. I almost wanted to giggle because his beard is tickling me.

Kissing. Touching. Moaning. Mr. Black led the way until we reached his bedroom. The lights are still off but it was dim rather than dark, thanks to some sconce on the walls and the windows that are large enough to welcome illumination outside. We fell on the bed with our lips still battling.

"It's time to take this off." He whispered seductively into my ears and started to unbuckle my belt. Although unintentional for him, but the way his fingers brushes into my skin, especially his knuckle hair made gasp for more air. Mr. Black dragged my pants down so easily. I felt the air cool down my impassioned body, awareness stopping this intimate daze for a second. Should we really do this?

Absolutely not. I heard my mother saying at the back of my mind.

"Wait! Stop." I put my hand on his chest. He stopped. "I really don't know if we should do this." I said.

Mr. Black smirked smugly. "I don't think so." he stared at my underwear which has now a wet spot on the middle.

"You just broke up with your girlfriend, sir." I said. He tensed for a moment before glaring at me with his eyebrows pulled down together.

"I told you to call me Magnus." he commanded and pulled my legs to make me sat on his lap. I can feel his erection poking from his pants. He then wrapped his arm around my back to carry me closer to him. "Say it." he murmured.

"M-magnus." I faltered. He smiled widely.

"That's right." He landed a kiss on my neck. "And do you know the reason why I got extremely irritated at the bar?"

"Madison broke up with you?"

"Wrong." another kiss.

"Hector cannot attend the meeting?" I guessed.

"Wrong again."

"Then what is it?"

"I saw you kissing that woman." after saying that, he lightly bit my ear. "You've been a bad employee... and for that you should be punished." he whispered before resuming to crush my lips.

"You know I really did that because a guy asked me out on a date." I don't know why I needed to explain what happened that night but his lips are hypnotizing.

"Shh. Stop making me jealous." he chided.

I already made the decision of surrendering myself to him. The hell with it. I'm liking this and I should stop denying it. I started to respond with much aggressiveness-- an expression of my repressed emotion trying to claw their way out of my memories. I stopped when he ceased to participate in my newfound ardor.

"What?" I asked him."Isn't this what you wanted? To stop.""No. It's not.""Then what do you want?"

I stroked his chest. I can't believe I'm saying this.

"You."

He smiled when he realized he won his game. The devil finally managed to capture the soul of the innocent.

"Do you?" he taunted.

"Yes."

"Prove it."

I pushed myself closer to him. "You already know the answer."

"I don't."

"I want you, Magnus." I whispered flirtatiously to his ear. He suddenly went stiff at the mention of his name and I grabbed the chance to lay him down on his bed. I started to unbuckle his belt but he stopped me.

"Getting a little too excited Mike?" he said.

Mike. The mention of my name struck me. It's no big deal since almost everybody calls me Mike but somehow when he said it, I remembered someone I drove away that day in the rain.

"Do you really want me Mike?"

And that afternoon under the tree...

"I do." I replied, entranced with the way he looks at me.

"Good. Because you are officially mine." with a conceited grin he owned my lips. The beast finally seized his victim and I took a bite at the forbidden fruit. "Remember that."

CHAPTER 19

I don't know why but I know that the house is calling me. Although the color is the same, you can notice the peeling of the paint which degrades its once glamorous facade. Here I am, standing outside our old house in Carmona Rosa. It's been years since I've step foot in this compound but I still know all the details of our old home. This house holds the majority of my memories naturally because I grew up here. I can still recall the way I've messed up the fence, the day I have left a permanent stain on the floor and the time when I scraped the banister out of sheer boredom. Like I said, I can still recollect even the tiniest detail from my past but there are some memories that I chose not to remember.

I proceeded to move forward towards the door, the stair creaking with every step. Before I could even knock, the door opened by itself as if it was awaiting for my return.

"Welcome home, son." I heard a woman's voice from a distance.

"Where are you?" I called out.

"In my favorite spot, if you can still remember."

I made my way out to the rear porch through the back door of the kitchen.

"Hello, mother." I said once I saw my mother sitting on her favorite rocking chair.

"I'm surprised you haven't forgot where it is." she sneered.

"How can I forget when you're always on my mind."

She stopped rocking her chair. "Really?" she asked, her voice mocking.

"Yes." I replied almost in a whisper.

"I've been warning you but you choose to ignore them."

"I didn't."

"You just did." she smiled bitterly. "You killed me Mike. You killed me." she said and started to sway her chair again. Back and forth and back and forth. All I did was watch and every time the pace gets faster, I can see her face getting older by every swing. She was laughing hysterically while her hair turned to white and her flesh started to rot. I just stood there watching in horror as my mother transforms herself into something frightening. In a blink of an eye, she was already in front of me holding my face, forcing me to stare at her decaying body.

"Don't you get it? Because of you, I never got the chance to grow old. I turned to this!" she kept screaming.

"No!"

I woke up just in time before I can even know what happens next. I sat up to pant for some air and wipe the sweat from my forehead. My dreams are becoming more vivid and it's a bad thing. I can still feel the touch of my mother's hand on my face.

I made a mistake. And now I must pay for it.

I looked beside me and I saw Mr. Black peacefully sleeping. I felt myself wanting to cry but I tried my best to hold it back. I did not regret what happened tonight but I feel disappointed with my self. I gave in to my desire. I broke my own promise. I lost.

"Hello, Mike." I slowly gaze up with fear when I heard my mother's voice call me even when I am no longer dreaming.

"H-how did you?" I asked in disbelief.

"Didn't you miss me?" My mother is here. With us. Sitting at the edge of the bed.

"You're dead!" I hissed.

"Yes, but in a way I'm not. I'm just a figment of your imagination or if I can guess, a product of your own conscience." I glared at her. I must be going crazy seeing my dead mother in the flesh in the middle of the night.

"Don't look at me like that. You're the one who brought me back to life."

"Go away!" I might have said that loudly so I looked down to make sure I didn't wake-up Mr. Black.

"I can't."

"Why?"

"You know why."

I was left staring at her. So real. Remembering my nightmare made my blood run cold. I left the bed and started searching for my clothes. I made my best to stay silent trying not to wake up Mr. Black while I dress myself up. I was about to say something to my mother but she is no longer at the bed or at the room with us.

I took a last glance at the naked man sleeping on the bed. This might be the last time I will be seeing him. Contented, I turned around and went out of the room before closing the door silently. This time, I'll do the right thing.

I went back to my apartment and packed everything I own. There's a high possibility that I will not be coming back here.

After that, I called a cab and instructed the driver to drop me off at Black Industries. There's still some things I needed to do before leaving the city. Thankfully the security officer granted me access when I said that Mr. Black needs me to get something in his office. I showed him my access pass when he got suspicious about my after hours visit. I assured him that I will not burn down his office or something.

The office is awfully silent when I got there. I got into his office and left my access pass and resignation letter I have written before leaving my apartment on his table. I stood there for a moment staring at the empty chair of my employer. I heard my phone ring. I took my phone out to check who was calling. It's Mr. Black. I hesitated for a moment whether or not to answer the phone. In the end, I answered it.

"Where are you?" asked Mr. Black with raging intensity. Even on the phone I can hear his heavy breathing and I can imagine him clenching his jaw in frustration with his eyes burning with rage.

"Goodbye, sir." I said and ended the call. He dialed again but I turned my phone off to avoid attempts of contacting me. I gathered all my personal belongings on my desk and prepared everything for my next successor. I made notes and endorsement on the planner for my unfinished tasks. After making sure everything's in order, I left the building with a heavy heart.

I thanked the guard for watching on my luggage. It took me less than a minute before I hailed another cab.

"Where to, boss?" the taxi driver asked me after getting into the cab.

"To the airport please. I'm going home."

Part 1/3 for the Mysterious Mr. Black is officially done. Now it's time for part 2. Are you ready for the past? Let's go visit Carmona Rosa and meet the parents... and Hector too! ;)

Chapter 20

This is a confession.

My name is Michael. I lived in Carmona Rosa ever since I was born until I turned seventeen. A lot of things happened when I was seventeen. It was our summer vacation and I had just finished junior high school. Usually kids my age would enjoy summer vacation by spending more time with their friends or having a part-time job. I, on the other hand is stuck here helping out at home because I don't consider this as a job since I am not getting paid. You see, we own a small bed and breakfast place for tourists and honeymooners who would like to visit the red river. Naturally I was asked to help run the business and I was bored for the whole summer break but something happened one night.

I was just about to lock the front door when I heard a loud crash outside. I took the key to the cash box and secured them to my pocket. Not that it contains a money anyway but it was the first thing that my instinct told me. My parents are asleep upstairs so I took the bat for self-defense in case a burglar is trying to break into our house. I carefully peeked behind the curtain from the sidelight of the door and was shocked to see a car crash outside. I immediately went outside and ran across the byroad towards the large oak tree where the accident took place.

There was a boy inside, unconscious with a bleeding head. Is he dead? I reached inside to his neck to look for some pulse but I jumped back when he opened his eyes.

"Are you alright? How are you feeling?" I asked. He just groaned placed his hand on the injured area.

"Please stay put while I call the ambulance." Before I could ran back inside the house he called me.

"Wait!"

I turned around and came back to his aid in case he needed anything.

"What?"

"Don't call the ambulance. I don't want any trouble. I'm fine. I just bumped my head on the steering wheel, that's all." he started to get out of the car and I assisted him until he sat on the ground and leaned on the car. It appears he's still dizzy.

"Are you sure? You're not in trouble with the law right. Or are you?"

"No! It's even worse if you call the police."

And now I get it. I can still smell the alcohol in his breath. He got into an accident because he's drunk.

"If that's what you want then fine."

He composed himself for a minute before opening his eyes again.

"Is this the bed and breakfast place?" he pointed at our house.

"Yes. It's our house." I replied.

"Take me there. I'll pay for my stay." I pulled him up and wrapped his arm on my shoulder to support him. We entered the house with much difficulty because he keeps on losing his balance and it's hard to carry a dead weight especially when you compare his body to mine.

I think I'll be skipping the registration and payment for tonight and just put him on one of the rooms. We usually don't practice express check-ins but what can I say, tonight is different. Instead of giving him the keys to the room first, I led him upstairs directly to one of the vacant rooms. I'll be using the master keys instead rather than getting the duplicate on the key rack because that would mean I have to leave and help him up again. That's just too much work for me because I really want to stop carrying his as soon as possible.

I opened the first room near the stairs and immediately laid him on the bed. I lifted his feet on the bed and helped him to be comfortable mattress.

"Would you like some water?" I asked him.

"Yes, please."

I went down to the kitchen and filled a pitcher with water. I also took a towel and a basin to wash his wounds. After I arrived to his room, I gave him a glass of water and went to the bathroom to fill the basin with water.

"Let me get that for you." I took the glass after he's done drinking and placed in on the table. He laid down again and closed his eyes in exhaustion. That's when I started to wipe the blood on his head. It took me three towel soaking and squeezing before his face was cleansed revealing a small cut on his forehead. I filled a cotton with a few drops of betadine before using it to disinfect the small cut. He flinched from the sudden burning sensation caused by the antiseptic formula.

"You know, you should really go to the hospital tomorrow to get yourself checked. You might feel okay for now you might have incurred an internal damage that will cause harm to you in the future." I advised him while I put the adhesive bandage on his forehead.

"I'd rather not." he replied.

"Why? I'm sure money is not an issue. I noticed your car looks expensive, so is your clothes." I rebut.

"I'd rather not talk about it." he then turned to his side like a moody teenager.

"Okay then as long as you're not a criminal on a run or a psychopath I respect your decision."

"Thank you."

"If you don't have any more injuries then may I know your name so that I can register it on the guest logbook." I stood up and got the basin and the towel.

"Hector." he finally replied after a series of heavy breathing.

"Hector what? I need to know your last name."

"Montgomery. Hector Montgomery."

"Okay. I'll leave you alone for now. We'll settle the other details tomorrow. Good night and I hope you'll have a great stay with us. Would you like me to turn off the lights before I leave?"

"Yes. Thank you very much." he said.

I then closed the lights before closing the door to his room.

Chapter 21

"So we've got a guest upstairs? There's some Hector written on the guest logbook." my mother asked me as she puts down the pan of eggs.

"We sure do. He's a last minute guest. Just in time before I closed the doors." I replied. "Oh and by the way, that's his car across the byway." I said and took a piece of bread and filled it with peanut butter as if that was a normal breakfast conversation.

"That crumpled red car?" my dad interjected.

"Uh-huh."

"What happened?" my mother asked with concern in her voice.

"I don't know really. I just went out after I heard a faint crash outside."

"I told you I heard a sound last night." my mother nudged my father to prove her point that she didn't imagined things like what my father used to say when she's paranoid. "I hope he's alright."

"Yeah. He's fine, just a little cut on the head."

"Such a shame for his car. It really looks expensive." my father chimed.

"Danny!" mother scolded him for his lack of concern. "Is he not coming down for breakfast?"

"I don't know. He's pretty tired last night." not to mention, drunk.

"Well you should send him his breakfast. It would be a waste if it would get cold." she prepared a platter of breakfast foods before handing me a tray of it complete with utensils and coffee.

"I don't think he would like to be disturbed." I reasoned out. I'm uncomfortable of barging in his room if he's still sleeping. That would be rude.

"Nonsense! This would make him feel better if he's exhausted last night." she really wanted me to bring his food upstairs that I have got no other choice but to carry the tray to his room. When I reached the front of his room, I took the tray down and knocked on the door.

"Room service!" I said in a loud voice. I don't know why I chose that word even though we're not in a hotel setting. It's really my first time bringing the breakfast to a room. Usually, the guest would come down to the dining area and we would be the one to serve them.

"Come in!" I heard Hector say inside. I opened the door first before carrying the tray up.

"Oh I'm sorry. Is this not a good time?" It looks like he just came out of the shower and he only got a towel wrapped around his waist.

"No, it's alright." he replied as he wipes his hair with another towel. I stood there like a frozen statue admiring his lean and muscular body. It just dawned on me that we had a young and attractive guest when I saw his body on broad daylight. Considering that he's rich too, I bet he is popular with the ladies.

"You can leave it on the table." he said when he noticed that I just stood there in the middle of the room. I shook my head to stop myself from further embarrassing myself and placed the tray on the bedside table.

"Thank you." he sounded cheerful today comparing to his self yesterday.

"You're welcome." I said before hastily leaving the room.

I continued to feast on my breakfast before returning to our mini reception area. I still need to charge him for his stay and I need to take an eye on him before he leaves. Not that I think he's gonna take-off and run but you'll never know. You really can't trust anybody.

Finally, I heard some footsteps coming down the staircase so I prepared the guest folio.

"Hector." I called him but he continued to walk towards the door. "Mr. Montgomery!" I raised my voice a bit and that's when I got his attention.

"Shoot. I forgot, I'm sorry." he went over to my side and dug into his back pocket for his wallet. "How much do I owe you again?"

I told him the cost. I heard him cursed beneath his breath. Oh no.

"Do you accept credit card?"

I knew it. He's gonna scam me with the I don't have any cash right now excuse.

"No. We only accept cash."

"Let's see, do you have any cash machines nearby?"

"The nearest cash machine is on the center of the town which is a fifteen minutes drive from here."

The floor started to shake, apparently from tapping his foot. The floor is made from wood that's why every repetitive movement such as tapping or jumping will be felt by the person nearby. He was thinking on his possible options and if he's thinking about running out the door, I'm gona swear to god he's gonna regret it.

"Then would you take my watch as a collateral?" he removed his watch on his wrist and gave them to me. It was a Rolex watch but I'm still not sure if it's genuine since I'm starting to doubt this guy's credibility. Common denominator for con-mans is that they use their good-looks to charm people. I will not be charmed even if he's got this magazine smile on his face. However, it seems like I still have no other choice but to accept his offer. If this turns out to be real then I'll be damned.

"I will keep this for the meantime. Now I need you to sign and fill up the necessary information on our guest folio." he only signed on the edge of the information sheet before handing them back to me.

"How about the address and contact number?"

"I'm too lazy to write it besides there's no need of that unless you need to reach out to me again."

"Fine, I'll write it for you."

"Thank you but I don't want to bother you."

"No, it's fine. I'm diligent when it comes to record keeping. Age?"

"Twenty-two."

Twenty-two, I wrote it on the data sheet.

"Address?"

"Hello good morning, is that your car outside?" my father interrupted us.

"Unfortunately yes, I lost control of the engine yesterday." Hector chuckled. BS. He's drunk that's why he had an accident.

"Well it looks like the engine's damaged. You might not use it for a while."

"I see. Do you know any mechanic here?" asked Hector.

"Yeah. If you want I'll call my friend Rick to take a look at your car."

"Yes please. I would appreciate it."

Father nodded and proceeded on the telephone to call Rick. Now where were we...

"Our son didn't mention we have a celebrity on our little home." suddenly out of the blue my mother appeared with the laundry hamper on her side.

"Thanks but I'm not a celebrity." he chuckled at my mom's remark.

"Are you sure? A model perhaps? Mike take a picture of our celebrity guest." she chided at me as a joke and it made me cringe so hard.

"By the way, if you need to get to the nearest cash machine, my father will be going to town to purchase goods. You can go with him." I inserted to the conversation before the topic will be changed again and everything will go astray.

"Maybe you should go with your father too Mike. Our guest might not know where to find the the nearest ATM" mother suggested. Translation: Keep an eye on him or I will whoop your ass if our guest will not be able to pay.

"Alright, I already called Rick. He said he'll come later to pick your car up." dad said to Hector. "And if you no longer need anything, I will be on my way now." he planted a kiss on my mother.

"Wait honey, the kids will go with you." she said.

"But I'm not done with the-"

She inspected the folio. "It's alright you can go."

"How about the address and number?"

"It's fine. There's no need for that."

"That's what I said." Hector mentioned and they proceeded to laugh for their newfound connection. From the looks of it, it seems like he already charmed my mother.

Chapter 22

S o since our car is a two-seater pick-up truck, Hector and I were cramped like sardines in a can. His big muscular body is my pushing my right side toward the door.

"Everything alright boys?" my father inquired.

"Yes sir." "Yep." we both replied at the same time. For all I know, that was just us being polite. I opened the window to let my arm out so that I can at least adjust for a little space. I knew I should've sat outside on the carrier.

"So where are you from Hector?" my father asked my seatmate.

"Um. Long Island." He answered but it's obvious that he hesitated sharing it at first.

"Long Island. Wow. No wonder you could afford that car. What brings you to Carmona Rosa?"

"I was actually on my way to meet some friends on California but then the accident happened."

The car stopped on a pedestrian and my father took the chance to talk further to our guest.

"But the main highway was 2 kilometers away from our town. You must be going the wrong way."

"It was late and I saw your sign so I decided to have some shut eye first. That's when my car slipped towards the tree." Hector replied.

Liar! He was drunk that's why he crashed his car.

"Yeah. You got to be careful since our roads gets slippery with mud after it rains. It rained like cats and dogs yesterday you know."

"I guess I didn't see how much mud there is since it was dark yesterday."

I still don't get it why he does not want to tell the truth. He's being dodgy with his answers.

"You know you could still take a bus to the airport and catch a plane to your friends. Then you can come back here once your car is totally repaired." my father suggested.

"No it's alright. My trip was supposed to be an adventure. I'm sure this is just a little detour before I can continue on my journey. Plus I just can't leave my car behind. I love that baby too much that I got to drive her until I reach my destination."

"If that's the case then you can have a little side trip on your own. Perhaps my son could take you for a sight-seeing." I stared at my dad for his unannounced volunteerism on my part. Say what now? "We've got beautiful sceneries here. I'm sure you would enjoy them as much as California."

"I'll think about it. How much time would you think it would take until I can ride my car back?"

"We'll it depends on what Rick would say. I'll give you his number if you want."

The crossing was cleared and we went right towards the town's parking lot. "Look for an open spot will you son." my father asked and I surveyed the area for an available space.

"Your favorite spot is available." my father nodded and parked the car in front of the trolley bay. I immediately opened the door and stretched my body while Hector talked to my dad for Rick's phone number.

"I'll be quick at the supermarket after that I'll visit the hardware store. Mike, keep our guest entertained" my father said before entering the store.

"So where's the nearest ATM?" Hector asked me with his boyish little smile.

"Follow me." If he ever attemted to run, I swear he will regret it for the rest of his life. We walked for a while until we reached the ATM on the other side of the building.

"I just have to make a call before I withdraw." he said.

I smiled, but in a sarcastic way which was not obvious. "Sure."

He dialed a number. "Hello? Is this Rick?" Rick, as in my father's friend Rick? "This is Hector the owner of the red car which I believed you have already picked up?"

But why would he need to call Rick?

"Listen um, based on you assessment, how much would I owe you just to get my car at the earliest possible time?...Uhmm Money is not a problem for me. I'll pay you extra just to make it done at the least possible time.... How much? ... Okay. Not a problem. Bye" and he hang up.

"He's a nice fella." he said to me. Probably because I still got my confused look on my face. "Okay, so where were we?" he rubbed his hands together before inserting his card on the machine. I was still watching him closely but he looked at me back.

"I need you to look back."

I knew it. He's trying to run away. And to think that he almost fooled me with his phony phone call. "Why?" I demanded.

"I don't want you to see my pin code." he said. I scoffed. As if I had the intention of robbing him when all I ever did was accommodate his request with not much questions.

"Fine. Three seconds." That should give him enough time to input his pin. He nodded and I counted from one to three before I turned back again. Interestingly enough he was still there. A few minutes later and a whole bunch of money was coming out on the ATM.

"What?" he asked. "You looked surprised?"

"Did you just robbed the bank?""No. Why would you even say that?"

I pointed towards the stack of cash in his hand.

"That's a lot of cash Hector." and it screams suspicious.

"I know but Rick asked for a downpayment. I would have withdrawn more but my card already reached its maximum daily withdrawal so I guess this will have to do." he replied casually.

"Yes. Thank you for mentioning the daily withdrawal limit. Isn't that like 300$ or 500$. Yours appeared to have exhausted all our reserves on the central bank."

"Not to sound arrogant but I think that depends on the bank and what type of account you have. If your average daily balance is high the bank is more likely to give you perks like a high withdrawal limit."

I wanted to roll my eyes but I know it will make me look like a sore loser. Fine, he's legit rich and it's not fair because he already has some good genes.

"Now, how much do I owe you again?"

I told him the cost. He counted from his money and gave some of them to me.

"That's a week's worth of stay. I guess I will be staying until I get my car back."

I counted the money. "Okay." It was the most money we received for this week.

"I'm hungry." he said.

"But you just ate."

"I know but I'm craving for something. Would you like some ice cream?" he pointed toward an ice cream truck on the opposite road.

"Sure. As long as you're paying." I feel like he's more of the guide here than me. We crossed the road and stood behind rowdy little kids.

"What do you want?" he asked me.

"Bubble gum."

"I don't think they sell candies here."

"No. I meant bubble gum flavored ice cream." I pointed at the menu to prove that I'm not making it up.

"What? Is bubble-gum a flavor now?" he sounded genuinely surprised.

"It's always been an ice cream flavor sine I don't know... the fifties."

"Hmm. Interesting. I didn't know that."

What kind of an adult does not know a bubble gum flavored ice cream? His spoiled ass looks amazed at the newfound concept that bubble gum is an ice cream flavor too. I thought he would be ordering one too but he went with the chocolate and nuts instead.

"Thank you." I said when he handed me mine.

"So where do we go now?" he asked me.

"I guess we can take a walk while we wait for my father to be done with his purchase." this time I led the way and showed him the parts of our town. He was actually a nice companion. I'm ashamed I misjudged him. Yeah yeah. I've got my own prejudice with attractive people cause they're always the popular ones in school and most of them are the mean ones but I guess he's one of the exceptions.

"What does it taste like?"he pointed at the ice cream I'm holding.

"I don't know. Gummy?" I don't know how to describe the taste.

"Let me have a taste." without a warning, he licked a part of it. I should be disgusted but I just stood there in shock as I observe him tasting the flavor.

"Hmm. Not bad."

"Yeah." I replied. You're not so bad yourself.

CHAPTER 23

"Let me help you with that." Hector offered when he saw me carry the grocery bags all at once. I think it is a universal law that it is better to suffer from carrying a bundle of grocery bags all in one trip than return again but with shame.

"No. It's alright. I got this."

I most certainly do not got it. One of the bags gave out and now several goods are on the ground.

"Thank you." I said when he started to pick up all that fell on the ground.

When we both entered the house, I thanked him once again and started to sort the supplies while Hector went back to his room. After finishing my task, I returned to the mini reception area and amended his records. The payment, I gave to my mother.

"So where's our guest now?" my mother asked.

"I think he's upstairs." I replied.

"Doing what?"

I shrugged. "I don't know."

"Listen, why don't you go upstairs and invite him for a little trip." she suggested.

"But mom. He might be resting." or doing something I don't like to witness if you know what I mean.

"Nonsense! And what do you think he might be doing upstairs. He decided to stay here for the week, I don't think he would love to spend it all week inside his room." as usual, before I could contest to her request, she started pushing me up the stairs.

"You don't know that. Maybe he likes to spend his time in private. Who knows, he might be doing a guy thing you know."

"Come on now, don't be silly." she shook her head but then whispered sometime later. "Knock if you have to."

"Fine. Just stop pushing me." my mother smiled with her victory and waved goodbye before disappearing in sight.

Here we go again. I knocked three times and waited for his response.

"Yes?" he said

"Can I come in?"

"Okay."

I turned the knob and found him busy with his personal belongings.

"Do you want to get out for a while. I could be your guide." I offered.

"Sure. I'll just arrange my things and then we'll go." he said.

"Where do you wanna go?" It was a stupid question since he was new here but I wanted to know if there was something else on his mind before I can show him what Carmona Rosa has to offer.

"Do you know where I can find Rick? I gotta hand him the downpayment first."

I nodded. "Uh-huh."

"Okay then. Let's go." he changed his outfit into a simpler one. We said goodbye to my parents before heading out on our way to Rick's Auto Shop which is a ten minute walk from here. I took a glance at the man beside me and it looks like he's got no intention of starting a conversation and so I took the initiative.

"What will you do in California?"

"Why are you curious anyway?" he said.

"If I'm being honest, there's still something about you that isn't quite right. I feel like you're not telling the whole truth."

He stopped from his tracks. "May I ask why?"

"I don't know. You refused to be admitted to a hospital when you are obviously in need of medical care." He looked at me in the eye, observing if he could trust me.

"I told you, I'm seeing some friends in California and we're supposed to go to Cancun for our spring break. Go to a casting call in LA if I'm in the mood."

"So you want to be an actor?"

He sighed and put his hands inside his pockets. "Not really no. But it pays a lot if I wanted to be independent."

"You ran away?"

He laughed. "No! I told you I'm on a spring break. You know what, why don't we walk a little faster. The sun is killing me."

We continued on walking until we reached the auto repair shop. Rick and Hector talked or a long time about his car, the cost, the repairs, parts needed and timeframe. I kept myself entertainted by watching one of the guys cover a primed car with paint. I never noticed that they're done talking until Hector tapped my shoulder.

"It's almost lunch, any recommended diner nearby?"

"Does that mean your treating me to lunch?" That sounds leechy. "Cause I don't have cash right now, I'm just saying." except for that five dollars at home.

"Don't worry. If I asked you for something, I'm paying."

My broke ass self was celebrating internally. It's a one of a lifetime experience to have a wealthy guest, might as well take advantage for it. I chose my favorite diner which I only dined for a handful times since my parents would often choose the cheapest available resto in town.

"What's the best meal here?" he asked.

"Their specialty fried chicken meal, which is what I would take please."

"Okay. Make that two please. How about your drink?"

"Uhhhmm..." I mumbled as if I was looking at the options but in actuality I expected him to ask that and I already prepared my answer. "Ice tea would do."

He smiled and gave the menu to the waitress. "Then that makes two fried chicken meal and two ice tea."

The waitress repeated our orders and tried to offer some specialty of the day. Hector declined and she left us but I heard her giggle as she walks away. My hunch was now confirmed-- she's having a little crush on my companion. I noticed that when she was repeatingly tucking her hair behind her ear while she was smiling so widely with eyes intently focused on Hector. I've never encountered a waitress so joyfully dedicated in her job before so I guess that concurs my conclusion.

"Is your name really Hector Montgomery?"

He raised his eyebrows. "Yeah. What about it?"

"It doesn't suit you. Sounds like a made up name if you ask me."

"Blame my parents if you want to." he then proceeded to take a sip on the glass of ffree water.

"Hector... Hector... There's something I about it." I thought about it for a second and a silly thought appeared on my mind. "Hector... sounds like a pornstar name."

He almost spilled his drink when he snorted. "Are you always this blunt to strangers?" he asked me.

"Maybe?" I admitted. "My classmates sometimes tell me to shut my trap when I observed something they don't want to hear."

"Is that why you got no friends?" he shot back.

I gasped a little. I knew he meant that as a joke but what he said stings a little. "I don't know." I whispered. "I was always the weird kid in class. I guess, I lack the social skills since our home is far from town and I'm the only teenager in our limited neighborhood."

"Oh, I'm sorry. I didn't-"

Just in time, the waitress came back with our orders. Good. A distraction from the awkwardness that now surrounds the table.

"Look, I'm sorry. I didn't mean what I said. That was a tasteless joke. Hector apologized after the server was gone.

"I know and it's okay since you're paying for this glorious food." I seized the cutlery and took a bite of my anticipated meal. "Now that's what I'm talking about."

We have already left the diner and we are already home but I noticed that Hector is still staring at me once in a while. It's making me self-conscious that I decided to confront him. "What?" I said.

"You know... I was thinking about what you said earlier."

"It's fine, really."

"If you want I can be your friend." he said. We both stopped walking.

"Come on now. I don't want your pity friendship. You're our guest and I'm okay with that."

"I mean it. You seem like a nice person."

"Now this is awkward but um after a week, you'll be out again on your own and I will be here on my own. In the second week, we both have forgotten that we even encountered each other. So to save the drama, let's remember, you're our guest and I'm one of your host."

Hector shook his head and laughed in disbelief.

"You know, you could gain more friends if you would stop being cynical. I really do want to be your friend and I promise you, I won't forget about you. You basically helped me last night and I'll always remember that. If you want, I will call you once in a while or someday I'll come visit your place again and then we'll have lunch with your favorite meal like an old friend. How about that?"

He sounded sincere with his words but the eyes tell more and I knew he was telling the truth. His eyes were one of his best asset, piercing but full of warmth. So alluring you could practically stare at them all day long.

"Okay." I said.

"Now that wasn't so bad isn't it?" he said then placed his arms around my shoulder like old pals. It made me uncomfortable at first since I'm not used to other people touching me but I found myself smiling for the rest of our walk.

It was the first time I made a friend. He promised not to forget about me and I know I should have done the same but sometime later, I was the one who have forgotten about his existence. Not until now that I'm thinking about what went wrong a week later.

CHAPTER 24

I was taken back to present when a hand wrapped itself around my arm. "Hey are you alright?" my seatmate asked me. I looked around me and I'm still on the train. There was no available ticket at the airport and I took the train home as an alternative. By the looks of it outside, there's still hours left on my ride.

"Hey. Are you alright?" my seatmate asked again, looking more concerned.

"Why? What's the matter?" I asked. She pointed at my face. "Is something wrong?" I used my left hand to navigate my face, searching for anything alarming. My cheeks were wet. Did I cry without me noticing it?

"Yeah. It's fine. I just remembered something." I said to stop here from worrying.

"A sad memory?"

I wiped my face using my sleeve. "Maybe. It's what I'm trying to find out."

I looked outside the window. My penance starts now. I shall once again revisit that buried part of my memories no matter how much it would hurt me in the end. Confusion. Regret. And most importantly, guilt. I'm guilty of something that isn't exactly my fault. Or is it? I need to remember so that I can make a verdict. Because if I am truly innocent, why is my conscience bothering me?

"Do you still want to explore more what Carmona Rosa has to offer?" I asked Hector when we reached our house.

"I think I'll pass. I'm tired from all that walking."he said.

"Good. Me too." It was just three in the afternoon and I think he can't do much in his room so I decided to invite him to our living room even though it is usually off-limits to guest. "Hey, if you got nothing to do, you can watch TV with me."

"Sure. I can do that."

We watched a movie in one of the channels and shortly after the film was done, my mother called us for dinner. Since he was our only guest, we invited him to join us for dinner. My parents mostly did the talking and after supper, we went back to the living room to watch more TV.

My father followed us afterwards "Is NCIS on?" he asked. It was his favorite TV show even though I don't understand the appeal of it. I changed the channel to CBS but it's currently on commercial.

"Hey Hector, Harvard, Upenn, Yale or Columbia?" he asked our visitor.

"That's stereotyping." he replied.

"Maybe. Maybe not. You look like the type that goes to an ivy league school. Am I wrong?"

"I say dropout!" I butted in. Hector stared at me offensively. "If it makes you feel better, most billionaires are college dropout."

"Harvard." he said as he looks at me to prove his point that I'm wrong.

"I knew it. Believe it or not, I was once a student in Harvard too." my dad replied.

"Really dad? You went to Harvard?" I said sarcastically. I knew my father was smart but Harvard smart? My father has told a thousand lies and I'm calling that this is one of his fabricated dinner conversation.

"Yes, I did. I'm a dropout but I'm not a billionaire." funny how my father never mentioned his college life and where he got the money to study there. "Is the old man Carver still there?"

"Yep. Still talking about supply and demand."

"If you see him go tell him to go fuck himself."

I choked. I didn't expect those words to come out of his mouth.

Hector grinned. "I certainly will."

"And tell him that I didn't cheat on his class. I've read the whole book thanks to his boring ass." my father added to his rant. There is certainly a deep seated hatred for that man I didn't even know.

"Dad, please don't take this the wrong way. Were you expelled from school because you cheated?" No wonder he never mentioned going to Harvard in college.

"Allegedly cheating." he corrected. "Shhh! It's already starting." he shushed me because NCIS is back in broadcast but I knew he does not want to talk about it so I dropped it. After the program was done he left and said that he's going to bed.

The TV is already our but there was nothing interesting to watch. Hector probably got bored because when I glanced at him, he was arms crossed with his eyes closed.

I don't know what took over me but I ignored whatever is playing on the TV and decided to take a good look at his face. Darn it. He is perfect. His faced is carved to perfection for the whole world to see. It's a sin not to stare.

Then I felt my heartbeat getting faster and faster. There's an indescribable warmth spreading through my body.

Suddenly, he opened his eyes and I immediately turned my eyes away from his.

"Were you staring at me?" he chuckled. A wide grin on his face.

There's no point denying it. He caught me and I can imagine myself being flustered right now. "Yes." I said but then an excuse appeared on my mind. "But only because you were snoring."

"I don't snore."

"Yes, you do."

He yawned. "I think I'm going to hit the sack." he said.

Yes! Crisis averted.

"Yeah. Okay. Good night." I said.

He stood up and shook the dirt on his pants. "Good night." He replied and went on his way to his room.

I was left staring at the television screen but my mind was running somewhere else. After a realization that I wasn't watching anymore, I turned the TV off.

Follow me: @therandomantic

Chapter 25

The priest was doing his sermon but I was spacing out the moment we sat down for homily. My mother who was a devout catholic lightly slapped my leg twice to revert my attention back to God. I fixed my position to make it seem like I was listening intently to the priest but my mind was still in other place.

Hector was left at the house. It was amazing really that my parents entrusted him a key to our house in case he would decide to go somewhere else.

What happened last night was still replaying in my mind. There is something about Hector that wants me to be closer to him. Charisma is truly oozing from his body and his visitation has offered some interesting moments from my humdrum life.

The mass ended and after having a brief conversation with their friends outside the church, we were finally on our way back home which made me indeterminably exhilarated. I must have been bored for far too long that I want to spend my time to this excitement as much as possible until it last.

When we reached home, I acted casual but I was the first one to get off the car. I twisted the doorknob to open it but it was locked.

"Oh honey. Let me get that." my mother offered and used her key to open the door.

I was disappointed to see no one in the house. Hector is not here right now. Why did I even expect. He probably got bored at home doing nothing.

I went to my room and decided to do what I think is one of my talents which is drawing. I convinced myself that I did it to improve my craft but I knew deep inside that I chose to draw because my desk is in front of the window wherein I can anticipate our guest's arrival. Once in a while I would crane my neck to check if he already arrived.

I saw someone getting nearer our house but he was on a bike. Is that him? I looked closer to investigate. It is him! Where did he get that bike?

I jumped from my seat and ran downstairs feeling like Christmas to welcome him.He was just steeping out of the bicycle when I reached him.

"Nice ride. Where did you get it?"

"Well... I went to by to Rick's to see how my car's doing and since it's punishing to walk from this sweltering heatwave, I decided to buy this second hand bike so I can use it to go back instead of walking." he replied.

"Are you still up for a trip to the lake?" I asked. I really hope would say yes.

"Sure. Can I have a glass of water?"

"I'll just get some supplies and I'll be back." I went to the kitchen to get us some sandwiches. I also grabbed some camping stuff.

After packing everything in a small string bag, I went out back to bring out my bike. I found Hector resting on our porch. I gave him a bottle of water.

He looks at my bike with amusement. "Cool. You also have a bike. I expected we would be walking again."

We rode on our bike and off we went to Lake Calico. The large and tranquil lake at the end of the river which is also one of the hidden gems of Carmona Rosa.

"This is nice." Hector said, sincerely entranced by the brilliantly blue water.

I parked my bike to a nearby tree. "Did you know that it was named Calico lake because if you would observe the lake at a distance it looks like it has three colors?"

"Really? What colors?"

"Red, brown and blue. The reddish hue is located near the river where the water reflects the trees. Blue pigment created by the sky where the water's deep and lastly, the color brown. Thanks to our clear waters the rocks and ground is visibly seen." I pointed at the different parts of the lake. "If you think about it, it represents three layers of the earth: the ground, the plants and the sky."

"So it looks like a three striped flag in the distance?"

"Not really. More like a mottled colored lake which resembles a calico cat. The ground is not evenly leveled so the colors are all smeared on this body of wat... er" I stopped talking when I saw Hector remove his shirt.

Right now he is now unbuttoning his short. I somehow lost my words when I saw his body. The only thing left is his boxer briefs. Unfortunately for my prude conservative eyes, the partial nudity fried my brain it damaged my speech and motor skills. The only thing I could do is gape at at the live stripshow.

"You talk too much. We're here to swim right?" he winked and dived straight into the lake. A splash of water to my face brought me back to my senses.

Once he rose from the water, he beckoned me to join him. "The water feels great Mike! Do you really want to spend the day under the sun? Or don't you know how to swim? It's easy, I can teach you "

I stood up. "Please. I'm the best swimmer in town!"

Unlike him, I only took my shirt off. The shorts can stay. I dived and felt the water cool down my sweaty body. "Now, watch me go."

In an attempt to impress my companion, I swam as fast as I can away from the dock to prove that I am not afraid to go to the deeper part of the lake which was probably a bad idea since I began to feel a contraction on my calf. I stopped kicking my legs to alleviate the pain that is now spreading around my hamstring. I tried to swim with one leg but I found myself sinking.

The pain was not subsiding and I can't lift my mouth underwater to yell for help. With panic arising, I used my arm to signal for help. Desperately pushing my other arm and leg and my body fighting for every last bit of air, body exhaustion took place. I felt myself being dragged down to the darkness below.

As foolish as I was, Death was on my side. Strong arms enveloped themselves underneath my underarms and began to drag me back to shore. Familiar with rescue protocol, I calmed myself to prevent ourselves from drowning together.

When we finally reached shore, Hector let me go and plopped himself to the sandy ground. "So much for the best swimmer in town." he said after he caught his breath.

I covered my face in embarrassment. "I'm sorry my leg cramped."

He sat up and removed my arm from my face. "Which leg?" he inquired and straightened my legs parallel to each other. I almost gasped when I felt his touch.

"The other one." I whimpered. He started to massage my leg but instead of the knot loosening, I started to froze from his gentle rub.

He looked at me sympathetically. "Hey. Try to relax. Your muscles won't ease up if you're being stiff." he cooed.

What he didn't know is that, I can't relax with him caressing me. The touch of his skin is sending sparks all over my being. As I look at his muscular torso while he massages my leg, I noticed myself burning up, breathless and becoming fervid with every touch; especially when I remembered how his body felt pressed against mine at the time he was pulling me back to shore.

Out of the blue, a silly thought started to germinate in my brain. I tried my best to stood up even though the pain has yet to wane. "I think I'm fine now. Thank you very much." I mumbled and started to walk, enduring the bolts of suffering in every step.

"Where are you going?" he opposed.

"I'm starting to feel cold. I'll get my shirt."

"But the weather is ridiculously hot."

"You can go back to swimming if you want to."

I didn't know why I lied. I'm flaming but yet I feel naked.

I started to tremble. This is bad. This is really bad.

Chapter 26

The way back home was awfully quiet. I didn't initiate to start a conversation and Hector sensed that something was wrong but he just went along with my silence.

I didn't slept well that night. I was pondering about something that I never discussed with anybody except my mother.

The next day, we were stuck at home due to heavy rains. Hector and I were still at a minimum interaction. He chose to spend the day watching TV while I decided to isolate myself in my room sketching random subjects to pass time.

Of course the lack of activity in the house will make anyone search for anything interesting to entertain oneself. Hector chose to explore the house until he decided to visit my room.

"What are you doing?"I heard him ask behind my back.

"Drawing… things." I replied.

I heard him walk towards me until I sensed him towering behind me. The next instant I felt his presence beside me. It seems like he was just fresh from the shower since I can still smell the whiff of minty soap emanating from his body. The hairs on my back started to rise when I felt the blow of warm air touch my skin with his every breath.

He leaned closer to take a peek of what I'm sketching, our heads almost touching. "Can I have a look?"

The extreme closeness is bothering me. My breathing became unstable as if air was completely stripped off the room. It's weird. I was getting warm but I'm starting to shiver.

"What?" I asked pretending to be annoyed.

He sat on the chair beside my table and leaned his head to his arms that was crossed on the back of the chair.

"It's good."

"Thank you."

"Can you draw me. You know like a portrait?" he suddenly asked out of the blue.

"You know I've never really tried sketching a human person-" which is actually true because landscapes are usually the subject of my drawing.

"I could pay you if you'd like. You know, like a souvenir."

"-But of course there is always a first time of everything." I followed-up. Money. Always a good motivator for a lazy person.

"So how should we do this?"

"Just lie on the bed naked and imitate Kate Winslet in Titanic." I said as a joke but then the bastard decided to take my word seriously because he started to unbutton his shirt.

"What. Are. You. Doing?" I snapped.

"What do you think?" he answered slyly with a slight grin on his face.

He's hysterical!

"I was joking!" I almost screamed.

He let go at the hem of his shirt and tapped my cheek twice. "So do I." he said and winked beguilingly.

I rolled my eyes as a response then proceeded to arrange his chair near the window. I sat on the bed. "Just take a seat and pose however you want." I commanded him.

He did what I told him and I settled to make myself comfortable before starting to draw the outline of his face. He chose not to smile but it didn't make him any less attractive, in fact it made him more appealing. Damn attractive people.

It was going smoothly and unproblematic than I was expecting but when I finally reached the point of drawing his eyes, things started to feel awkward.

The moment our eyes met, I felt myself fluster. With every glance I took, I felt like I was being absorbed into the windows of his soul. My hands started to shake and I did my best to avoid committing mistakes by keeping my hands steady as possible to avoid shaky lines. Deep inside I wanted to scream my heart out but I didn't know why. Something inside me is going insane. This eye contact felt like something so intimate even though I have never been this connected to other people.

After what felt like a day, I was finally done with my portrait. I glanced at my drawing and I felt proud. It's not actually bad for a first timer.

I raised the portrait that I drew to show it to him. "Presenting to you, my Magnus Opus as of the moment." I declared. Instead of admiring my work he laughed.

I scowled at him. "What? Is this ugly? It totally looks like you." I swear I did good. I consider it my best drawing among all my art.

He chuckled for the second time but he stopped when he saw my offended expression. He shook his head to stop and looked at me amusedly. "Oh it's nothing, I just remembered something. If I say that's ugly then I'm also insulting myself. By the way, it's Magnum Opus. Not Magnus Opus, magnum is the Latin neuter singular nominative adjective form that means 'great' in English, while magnus is the Latin masculine singular nominative form for that means 'great' but should be properly used to describe a man."

"Whatever. Tomato-tomato. It means the same. Plus you're a boy so I think that makes me right."

"Not really, since opus is neuter in Latin, the correct phrase for a "great work" or "masterwork" in the form of, let's say, your art, magnum opus; is still the correct term in the strict literal sense. But if you would like the more accurate Latin term, it's opus magnum since adjective should come after a noun."

"Wow. And I thought I was the nerd in room."

"We studied Latin but that doesn't make me the dork in this room."

"K." I dismissed.

He tapped my shoulder gently. "Fine. You did a good job." he complimented.

And there was that spark again. Every contact he makes are electric. Is this really what I think it is? Am I starting to like this guy? This complete stranger who just stepped into our life out of nowhere.

The rain stopped and silence started to fill the room.

"D-do you want to grab a snack." I offered to break the awkward atmosphere that is beginning to surround us.

"Sure." he replied.

I scampered my way toward the door. I need to stay away from him. I just have to.

I looked back and I saw him standing still where I left him.

"Are you coming?" I asked.

There was a slight pause before he said: "Sure.", with a devilish smile plastered on his face. I felt my feet squirm inside my shoes. Somehow I can feel that he knows. I haven't been that subtle and my secret has been exposed.

EPILOGUE

Hector said he needed to buy some supplies so I accompanied him to town. My father even gave him permission to use the truck even though he cannot use his own car mainly because he crashed it while driving under the influence. My parents have been so trusting to a guy they just met while I, on the other hand needs to beg for their permission to go out during the weekends.

We were walking along the sidewalk when I saw Jessie and his boys strolling like they own the road. Jessie was the school bully and I was one of their favorite target to their maltreatment. I let my head down and faced the pavement hoping that none of them would notice me.

"Hey faggot, that your boyfriend or some paid callboy?" Alas! I was wrong. I bit my lip when I heard Jessie trying to provoke me. I chose to ignore him like I usually do but Hector decided to stop and entertain him. "The name's Hector and I'm not a callboy." he said.

Jessie snickered. "Hector? Like the pornstar? Then I'm right. You are a callboy." His minions cackled like laughing hyenas.

Hector was about to rebut him but I grabbed his arm to keep us from walking instead of wasting our time entertaining a human garbage. Things were about to end but then Jessie couldn't keep his mouth shut and persisted to annoy us. "Make sure to use protection or else you'll spread the gay virus."

In a swift moment, I heard the clattering sound of a metallic object. I looked back and saw Hector with a curled fist and Jessie lying on the ground with a crumpled trash can.

Jessie immediately rose and attempted to tackle my companion but Hector grabbed him by the collar and slammed him on the wall.

"What makes you think you can just spout offensive things from that dirty little mouth of yours?" Hector asked in a threatening manner. He must be clutching the collar of his shirt too tightly because Jessie started to choke while desperately trying to wiggle his way out from his grip. The minions just watched as their leader began to lose air.

"Do you think it makes you tough when you bully someone? Is that why you're doing it?" the minions and I just kept on exchanging glances since nobody knows what to do.

I saw Jessie turning blue but it looks like Hector has no plans on putting him down. "Hector, let go of him!" I screamed.

Finally, someone saw the commotion and yelled to call our attention "Hey!" we heard someone say.

"Hector, let's go!" I called and beckoned for him to run. Before the adult could come closer to the scene, we have already dispersed and went our separate ways.

Once we have reached a safer area, I stopped from my tracks and leaned both my hands on my knee to catch my breath. I heard Hector laugh beside me.

I glared at him. "What's funny?" I asked. He probably lost his mind.

"You shoud've seen the look on his face." he said in between his laugh.

"Yeah, you look like you're gonna murder him." To be honest I was also a bit scared because he suddenly became like a different person when he got angry.

"I was expecting for a thank you and you're welcome by the way, that guy won't bother you anymore." he answered casually.

I stared at him seriously. "What were you gonna do if nobody noticed us?"

"What do you think?" he returned the question back to me.

"I was asking you."

"Please" He dismissed. "It was just a harmless threat." I was about to rebut his statement but then he changed the topic. "Anyway, why does everyone thinks my name sounds like a pornstar?"

"Do you really wanna know?"

"Yes."

"Then follow me." I led the way and continued walking until we have reached the fiendish part of town where all sorts of illegal transactions usually occur.

"What the f-" Hector cursed when I pointed at an adult video store where the display window shows a cutout picture of a shirtless stud in a bad fireman costume. The name Hector was plastered all over the place from the abundant video collections to various novelty merchandise such as shirts and mugs.

"You see, your name is iconic in the adult video world."

He mumbled something incomprehensible.

"What's that?" I asked.

"I said do you wanna watch his films?" he then wiggled his eyebrows up and down.

"Eww, no." I said in disgust. Just as I looked behind his back, I saw a familiar face. Dammit, among all people I know I saw my most bigoted, racist, homophobic and the worst teacher I ever had. She once reprimanded me for having a dirty shoes and even managed to insult my whole existense because of a muddy sole. Today is my lucky day I guess. Two bullies in a row.

She was walking towards our direction and so I did the most reasonable thing to do, to flick her off.

Just kidding but how I wish. I, instead used Hector as a human shield to avoid judgement from my middle aged Karen of a teacher.

"What the heck are you doing?" Hector questioned. I held on his arms as a way to tilt his body everytime Ms. David got closer.

"Shhh!" I shushed him. I don't want my judgy teacher to see me standing in front of an adult video store. I know I'll never hear the end of it and she'll probably shame me for lusting over some pornographics materials which I did not even do. Also with the fact that she can't keep her mouth shut from spreading fake news during PTA meetings.

I heard her footsteps stop behind Hector. Holy fuck! She probably recognized me as one of her student and she wants to see the identity of her next town gossip topic. I buried my face in Hector's chest. I cannot let the old witch view my face. Hector didn't move and I'm thankful for that. With all the things that's happening, I finally noticed the faint smell of his cologne mixed with his natural odor which smells so masculine and nice. I felt my heartbeat accelerate and it's not because of fear but because of excitement. Realization hits me like bugs on a windshield.

I heard Ms. David express his disapproval by making a syllabic sound before finally moving on to her business while mumbling 'fucking faggots'. I estimated that she already left before I separated myself to Hector then I started walking away without saying anything, never minding which direction to take. I heard Hector call me but I continued on my way.

"Mike!" he yelled. He sprinted until he finally caught up with me. "You alright?" He asked with concern in his eyes.

I stared at him. Stop being so perfect, my mind formulated as a reply but instead, I just gaped like a total idiot.

"Hey Hector!" our attention was diverted when someone called him.

"Yes, Rick?" Hector replied. I looked down and grimaced behind their back.

"We're just finishing some parts on you car. You can pick it up anytime by tomorrow." I suddenly froze when I heard Rick mention that they're done with the repair. It dawned on me that even though I'm enjoying Hector's company, someday he will pack up and leave. I always despised it when someone you're used to seeing and talking will one day disappear from your routine. The after effects of missing someone usually last long especially when that person left an impression on you.

"I'll see to it that we're going through with our agreement." Hector said.

"So we'll expect you tomorrow?"

Hector glanced at me before answering him. "I don't know. Let's see."

Rick tapped his shoulder. "I hope we'll see you. We barely have a space in the shop right now." he said jokingly and laughed before going on his way.